Journey to Almost There

Also by JoAnn Bren Guernsey

Five Summers

Journey to Almost There

JoAnn Bren Guernsey

Clarion Books

TICKNOR & FIELDS: A HOUGHTON MIFFLIN COMPANY

New York

With special thanks to Willi Brennaman,
John and Ethel Gleason, Dr. Bruce Van Dyne,
and Dr. Felix Zwiebel.

Clarion Books
Ticknor & Fields, a Houghton Mifflin Company
Copyright © 1985 by JoAnn Bren Guernsey

Printed in the U.S.A.

Library of Congress Cataloging in Publication Data

Guernsey, JoAnn Bren.
Journey to almost there.

Summary: To prevent her grandfather's going to a
nursing home, Alison drives him from Minnesota to
Massachusetts, where her estranged artist father lives.
1. Children's stories, American. [1. Grandfather —
Fiction] I. Title.

PZ7.G9357Jo 1985 [Fic] 85-2685
ISBN 0-89919-338-2

P 10 9 8 7 6 5 4 3 2 1

To my husband, Ron, the truest of believers and dreamers, with gratitude and enduring love.

Journey to Almost There

Chapter 1

*F*IVE-THIRTY A.M. The baggage had been squeezed together in the trunk and back seat to make room for any stray sacks or afterthoughts. The last raindrops from the midnight storm hung from the giant white pine, heavy cold drops that stretched and waited to plop onto Alison's head, but she barely noticed. Running away was a sober business.

Lastly, after loading the car and wiping down the wet windshields, after searching every room of the house for forgotten necessities, she collected her grandfather. She knew he had taken his sedative later than usual that night; she had seen to it. He was groggy but not especially uncooperative. He helped her dress him, automatically lifting and shoving and trying to fasten. He mumbled, leaned on her, shuffled as best he could, but she knew he was basically asleep. He would not wake up until they were deep into Wisconsin.

His bony arm circled and dragged down her neck so that she had to stop four times between his bedroom and the car to shift his weight. Thankfully, Oliver was incredibly skinny, and she was, she knew, stronger than she looked.

She'd worked hard at gymnastics until she'd done the unthinkable — two years ago, at age thirteen, she'd shot up to five foot six, then five foot six and three-quarters. And her weight had actually dropped. Nobody wants a gangly gymnast, she'd been told. It was one of the few such facts of life she'd accepted gracefully.

Before settling in behind the wheel of the car, she gave the house one last look. Already she felt the distancing, and it was so pleasant that she took several deep satisfied breaths. She caught the dark fishy smell of unearthed worms. By midmorning when her mother reluctantly returned, there would be dozens of dead worms baking on the pavement. And, Alison thought, we'll be long gone.

The sky was opening and the clouds were beginning to drain behind the sun, which still spread fat and lazy on the eastern horizon. She started the car and smiled at her grandfather, who was snuggling against the car seat as though it were the plumpest down. He sniffed and smacked his dry lips. What was he going to say when he awoke on the road? Would he order her to turn back to Minneapolis? No, that wasn't his style. Besides, it was mostly because of him they had to leave.

The interstate highway stretched ahead endlessly. Alison could not believe she had been driving only two hours — every muscle in her body screamed to move. She'd been driving a lot since getting her permit (becoming, it seemed, the official family chauffeur), but only the back-and-forth, fifteen-minute-at-a-time variety of driving.

She tried to spot a familiar landscape, since she and her mother had driven this route a few years earlier, but there was nothing particularly reassuring. She couldn't even remember why they'd driven to Madison that time. Some kind of women's conference, she thought. Alison had been eleven and still trying to escape the Little League baseball her mother had been pushing at her for years. "Equal rights for women." Her mother used the slogan like a sacred vow, one which made Alison fearful rather than convinced.

All Alison was really sure of was that she wanted the same rights as everyone else, including the right to be lousy at baseball. And the right to spend vacations like other kids and not sitting through boring women's conferences. Why, she wondered, had she been forced to beg for years for one little doll? Just one? "I'm raising a fifties child," was her mother's favorite way of ending their arguments about such things.

Their blowup yesterday, however, had not ended that way; it had not ended at all. It had started with Alison's sudden infatuation with Raoul, a lippy sixteen-year-old dropout, and with her mother's overreaction to the idea.

Alison really didn't care that much about Raoul; she was drawn to him in an offbeat sort of way, the way she might want to reach out and pet an alley cat that hunted alone and smelled of people's garbage. But her mother's hatred for him gave him more charm than he could ever have possessed on his own.

"You're at it again, Mom," Alison had said when her mother had ordered the boy out of her house. (Right in front of her mother, Raoul had started kissing Alison's neck as if it were as natural a gesture as a smile.) "You're trying to tell me who I should like and dislike. Next you'll be telling me to stay away from So Poi — who isn't my own kind either, heaven forbid."

"So Poi is a lovely young lady whom we've known for years. The comparison is ridiculous." Her mother always stayed calm for a long time. Infuriatingly calm.

"The comparison is not ridiculous. You just can't see it when you get like this. You're prejudiced, that's what you are. And overly suspicious." Alison had been learning how to puncture her mother's calm with very little effort. "You, supposedly of the great sixties generation, all the race riots and peace marches and equality stuff — "

"Stop that," her mother spit out.

"Where's Raoul's place in your hippie picture of things?"

Her mother shook her head slowly. "Back to the hippies again, huh? I wish you would stop that." Still shaking her head, she closed her eyes. "I wasn't . . . I mean there was no . . . I *had* no generation. Not the way you mean." Behind closed eyelids her mother seemed to shut something off. When her eyes opened, only the anger remained, honed to an edge. "That boy is worthless and you know it. You treat a nice boy like Jordan as if he was no better than an insect and then you bring that . . . that *thing* here instead."

"Jordan, Jordan, Jordan. That's all I hear from you lately," Alison said. "If you like him so much, you can have him for yourself. You could probably order him around, like the other men you know."

"We're not talking about me. My judgment is not at issue here. It's yours."

"Jordan is nice, Mom. He's cute and smart and everything he should be, but . . ."

"But what?"

"He doesn't . . . I don't know . . ."

"Turn you on? Is that it? He doesn't make you tingle and quiver?"

Alison only glared at her for that. She wanted to tell her mother that, as a matter of fact, Jordan did turn her on in a way. But she doubted if her mother wanted to hear that either.

4

"And how about Raoul?" her mother continued. "Does he turn you on?"

Alison shrugged.

"Of course he doesn't. You're just being a child. A brat!"

"You're the one who's trying to keep me a child." Alison tried to ignore the hateful word *brat*. Her mother had never called her that before. "I'm practically a grown woman. I've been getting my period for almost two years. I'm . . . I'm – "

"If it's periods that give you maturity, young lady, then surely you're grown up enough to think of what else they can give you."

"Don't lay a bunch of pregnancy junk on me." Alison was practically shouting. "I'm not some dopey kid who doesn't know how to use contraceptives."

Alison's mother had lifted her hand then, as if to slap her. They both stared at her hand for a moment before her mother turned and ran out of the house. That upraised hand had made Alison all the more certain – she was going to Rockport.

Later, after Oliver had come home from his well-timed walk, her mother had called. Oliver had answered the phone and spoken very briefly to her. "She's at Sheila's," he'd told Alison. "A pajama party or something with some friends." He had chuckled as if the whole thing were a joke. But then, of course, Oliver couldn't have known about their fight. Not unless he'd been able to read Alison's mind.

"Pajama party, my foot," she had mumbled, but not for Oliver to hear. Okay, Mom, you've made it easy; we'll go tonight.

The car was humming so smoothly now that Alison almost envied it. When she relaxed her grip on the steering wheel, she noticed how she trembled, so she gripped tighter still. Her foot on the accelerator felt tentative. The radio would help, she thought, but then she glanced at her grandfather, still asleep in the seat beside her. "Wake up, Oliver," she said quietly. "I'm lonesome."

His eyes did not open, but the corners of his mouth pinched upward. He may have been drawing himself up from a pleasant dream, probably one of those in which he was thirty again instead of seventy-three and married instead of alone. Well, nearly alone. Alison felt guilty for interrupting such a dream and let him sink back. Better that she be lonely than that he be aware of where he was and what she had done.

The highway was straight for a good while, so after easing up on the accelerator and checking for any other traffic, she allowed herself several more quick looks at Oliver. There went the corners of his mouth again. A stingy smile, some would say, but the best he had, even awake. It hadn't been too long ago that he couldn't smile at all.

The early morning light dusted his pale eyelashes where they lay against the blue-black crescents under his eyes — reminders still of his long illness, as were the sharp cheekbones and chin. Hard angles. He was all angles, but the hardness was an illusion.

In spite of the fact that she was driving, Alison had a strong, early-morning urge to stretch across the seat to cover his forehead with kisses. Happy June, Grandpa. Happy summer. Happy freedom.

Perhaps he sensed he might have to fight off such an attack, because he opened his eyes wide and lifted his head. His ferocious sneeze made them both jump.

"Good morning, Oliver." She tried for a great, dazzling smile.

6

"What the hell . . ." He sat up quickly and looked around.

She let him look long enough to fully wake up and assure himself that, yes, Alison really was driving her mother's car and he was somehow her passenger. "We're going on a trip, Oliver. East."

"So it seems," he said, regaining his composure quickly, a special talent of his. "East, eh? How far east?"

"All the way," Alison replied. She gazed straight ahead, squinting into the sun, and realized that she'd been squinting so long that her face felt permanently shrunk. There was not a scrap of cloud left. "Can you find my sunglasses in that bag there?" She motioned with her chin and right elbow toward the lumpy tote bag between them, still avoiding a looser grip on the steering wheel.

He didn't move. "I've been kidnaped? Is that the idea?"

She looked at him, stifling a giggle. "So it seems."

"Kidnaped." He seemed to be trying it on for size as he halfheartedly began to rummage for her sunglasses. "You'd think they could come up with a better word for it," he mumbled. "For a person my age."

"How about grandpa-naped?"

"Stolen right out of my nice bed, the one I've spent years breaking in. Here they are." He handed the sunglasses across and looked at her as if for the first time. "But you're not supposed to be driving." He stated it without accusation.

"I'm fifteen, got my permit. You're a licensed driver, so what's the problem?"

"Not licensed anymore. I don't think. Am I?"

She shrugged. "Hungry? There's a box of food in the back seat."

He raised himself onto his knees to find what he wanted, but his body swayed uncertainly. "Haven't gotten my . . . uh, car-legs yet, I guess."

"I'll pull into the next rest area that comes along, if you like. But in the meantime, you can start eating. I know how hungry you are in the morning. I brought hard-boiled eggs, sweet rolls — almond, of course — and a thermos of hot tea."

"You've thought of everything. Been planning this long?" He was struggling to pour the tea.

"For a few days. Since before school let out."

"And I didn't guess a thing." He peeled an egg neatly and salted it too much with the tiny blue shaker she'd included. "Must be slipping," he mumbled before stuffing half the egg into his mouth.

"You're not slipping," Alison said. "I'm just getting better at hiding things from you." She looked at Oliver briefly. A few yellow crumbs of egg had been snagged by the gray bristles in his chin. She wanted to brush them off.

"Don't you think your mother might miss us?" he asked. "Not to mention her car."

"It was going to be mine soon. Mom said so, when I turn sixteen. Besides, she hardly ever uses it. She walks to the store, takes the bus to work, avoids driving as if someone's out to get her as soon as she backs out of the driveway. I never could figure her out. She's not supposed to be afraid of anything."

"According to who?"

"To her, of course."

"Well, a little fear never hurt anyone."

"Fear of driving a car is neurotic if you ask me," she said, shifting uncomfortably in her seat. "I'll admit I came a little unglued at first, since I've only driven around town before. But there's really nothing to it. Not with the Triptik."

"The what?"

"Triptik. Right there." She motioned toward the elongated

booklet of maps sticking out from under the tote. "See, each page is a small section of the map, enlarged and marked with a red line telling you where to go. You flip each page as you reach the end and start again on the next. It's as simple as following a recipe."

He flipped through the book and Alison could see out of the corner of her eye the red line zigging and zagging across the pages. She swallowed, aware for the first time what all of them meant in distance.

At the end, Oliver stopped and stared. "Springfield, Massachusetts?" He sounded totally bewildered.

"That's where the Gallaghers went." She was determined to sound casual now; if he was going to object, now would be the most likely time. "You know, Molly's parents. That's where I got all the maps and tourbooks. Molly smuggled them to me and I swore her to secrecy. We can trust her."

"But, what's in Springfield?" Oliver asked.

She sighed, exasperated. "Nothing. That's where the Gallaghers went, I said." She spotted the sign she'd been waiting for. "Next rest area, four miles. I'll bet you have to pee like crazy by now."

"Mind your own business . . . and while you're at it, please explain where we're going."

"Rockport. See it, way over there? On the ocean. There's an artists' colony there."

Oliver began to nod slowly and then smiled. "Your father. Of course. How dense can I be?"

She was encouraged by the tone of his voice. "I think Dad's going to settle there. He's been selling tons of his paintings, and he likes the scenery and the people."

"But your mother —"

"She doesn't know where he is. She doesn't care. His

letters are addressed to me and, since I get home before she does, she never sees them." Alison smiled. "I left false clues all over my room so she'd think we were headed west. A travel guide for California – hidden, but not very well. Lots of artists live there too, you know. Some scribbled phone numbers in my wastebasket, of travel agencies. Calls I actually made, by the way, asking for advice on how to drive to San Francisco from Minneapolis. Stuff like that. Not too obvious, though. I'm not dumb." My God, she thought. Did I remember to take every one of Dad's postcards and letters?

"Of course you're not dumb," Oliver said, spraying flakes of sweet roll in every direction. "Neither is she. What did you say in your note? You *did* leave a note, I assume."

Alison glared at him. "Of course I did. She'd have died of fright otherwise. But she doesn't know where we're headed."

"What happens when they torture the information out of Molly?" He sounded so serious, Alison had to laugh.

"Good Lord, Oliver." They laughed together, and Alison felt the muscles in her neck and shoulders begin to loosen. "Hand me one of those rolls, will you please? And a sip of tea? We won't be having lunch for a long time."

"Right, Chief." Oliver dumped egg shells and crumpled paper into the plastic trash bag she'd remembered at the last minute. He shook his head, chuckling, then he stopped suddenly. "Who the hell dressed me?" His hands flew to the zipper of his pants.

"Who else?" Alison grinned and turned on the radio. But he looked so genuinely distressed that she added, "You woke up enough to do most of it. Don't you remember?"

He shook his head, still covering his fly. "Must be slipping bad."

10

She glanced at him, but he was not serious; he needed no reassurance right now. I should be so lucky, she thought. If only I could tell him about my fight with Mom. But he'd only try to convince me that there's really no reason to be as terrified as I am right now.

Chapter 2

*A*LISON PULLED into the rest area and stopped. When she turned off the engine, the rumbling of travel continued just under the surface of her skin for a few seconds. The stillness was almost frightening, as if it were the rush of blood in her veins that she'd been hearing and suddenly there was dead silence.

Oliver groaned with relief and disappeared inside the rest room before she had even opened her door. Unbending her stiff body and limbs, she discovered a brand-new, sheer delight in standing up straight. Her backside was numb, flat feeling, and she wondered if, after this trip, she would always look as though the mold of a car seat had just been peeled away from her.

Oliver returned from the bathroom quickly, and his walk, she thought, had an extra bounce to it. He was having a good time. She needn't have worried about his reaction to the trip. He always had been adventurous.

"Much better," he called out to her, stretching clenched fists skyward. Very little of the stooped posture of his illness was apparent; he was almost tall. His shoes, she discovered, were on the wrong feet, giving the impression that he was headed in two directions at once.

"Sorry about the shoes," she said. "It was dark."

"I never knew I slept so soundly." He leaned against the car to switch his shoes around. "Didn't you worry that I'd wake up and raise hell?"

"Not really. Mom wasn't home anyway, and I know how groggy those sedatives make you. Remember the night the smoke detector went off for some reason and we tried to make you understand there might be a fire in the house?"

Oliver looked sheepish.

"Oh, it was understandable. But that night you never did seem to wake up. All you did was mumble something about Grandma and light switches and blankets. I'm not sure . . ."

To Alison's surprise, her grandfather blushed. His face tilted downward at an angle away from her, but she could see the red streaks rushing to his cheeks from his furrowed neck. He cleared his throat and inspected his shoelaces once more.

"Oliver," she said, careful to change the subject. (He was extremely sensitive about her grandma.) "You are looking terrific today. Better than I've seen you look in ages."

He bowed appreciatively.

"Why on earth Mom thought you couldn't be left alone all day, I'll never — "

"That reminds me, Chief. You remembered all my medicines?"

"Yes, of course. You're taking them late, aren't you? We'll have to watch that better from now on."

The back seat was neatly packed with everything but the luggage, which was in the small trunk of the car. Oliver took a quick survey of the back seat as Alison located his pills. "I see you remembered all the necessities: your art supplies, rain gear, sleeping bags – "

"And our recorders."

"Yes, two alto recorders, all the weatherbeaten old duet books your grandma and I used to use and, well, I assume there's something resembling clothing somewhere, and how about my shaving gear? Can't stand to – "

"Clothes are in the trunk, shaving stuff in the tote. Don't worry; I didn't forget anything. I even bought traveler's checks yesterday."

"With what money?"

"Yours from the cigar box – "

"How'd you know – "

" – and mine from the bank."

"Alison Kay O'Brien." He glared at her. "You didn't withdraw your college money."

"I'm not, as if you didn't know, going to college anyway. I'm going to get scholarships to art school. That's what I've always wanted. It's Mom who keeps talking about college. She probably thinks it will make me more of an activist or something."

Oliver poured more tea and took a pill, still looking upset. "It's not that you don't have the talent to get scholarships – of course you do, and then some. But I don't think you realize how much it's all going to cost."

"I'll work for a while. What's wrong with learning from . . . well, from life?"

"Like your father did?" He got back into the car and slammed his door.

"Why not?" She bent down to speak to him and noticed another new crick in her back. "Except a little more settled, a studio somewhere."

Oliver didn't appear to want to continue the argument.

His nose twitched violently. "Better take my sneeze pills, too," he said, rummaging through pill bottles again. He hummed a snippet of the Hallelujah Chorus — a technique he often used to suppress sneezes.

Alison sighed, relieved to have gotten the money part over with. Now there was nothing left to bring up, at least nothing she cared to think about at the moment. "I gotta go to the bathroom," she said as she strode from the car toward the small brick building.

After washing up, she considered combing her hair. But combing never seemed to produce much change; her hair's long, lank brownness had been effectively changed only once, when she had impulsively gone to a beauty shop for a permanent. Her hair had ballooned into a monstrous Brillo pad, giving her the choice of cutting it all off or wearing a football helmet (the only kind of hat heavy enough to control it). Her mother hated the curls so much she seemed to look past them for months. Alison, naturally, had pretended to like them just fine. "Nothing wrong with femininity," she'd said, as though it were a slogan of her own. But she was secretly relieved when the last brittle curl had been snipped off.

Her hair was straight and shoulder-length again now, not thin exactly, but somehow inadequate. And it was a shade lighter than during her childhood, which her mother attributed mysteriously to puberty. Running her fingers through it to free her neck from its stringy grip and resticking it behind her ears was about all she ever did to her hair except for combing it in the morning.

Her T-shirt (I ♥ Picasso) and blue jeans already seemed grungy, the careful soap smell of the morning left behind in the closet with all her dresses, pantyhose, and pinchy shoes.

Back in the car, she felt Oliver staring at her. His trusting but slightly frightened eyes prickled her skin and brought back the jumpiness in her fingers.

"I can't take it all in," he said. "I just can't. Did you tell me what on earth you said in your note?"

Alison considered telling him she'd already explained all that; sometimes she could get away with such evasion. But she took a deep breath. "I told Mom that we weren't running away, so she shouldn't call the cops. We're just going on a little trip, a vacation, I said. We'll be back soon. Not to worry, I've been driving a lot the last few weeks. Stuff like that."

"Is that true? About being right back?"

Alison gripped the wheel again. "Depends."

"If it depends on your father, don't — "

"Oh, yeah. I also told her to call that . . . that place she found for you and cancel your reservation or whatever you call it."

"It was a senior citizen residence, Alison. Nothing so hideous about it. Not really."

"Did you want to go?" She stared at him.

He turned to his window and scratched his cheek. The sandpaper sound gave her goose bumps. "No, of course not," he answered at last.

"Well, then."

"I just feel so responsible for this . . . for everything."

"She was gone all night, Oliver. Gave us the perfect chance, staying overnight with her 'girlfriends.' Why can't she act her age?"

"Don't be so hard on your mother, Chief." Oliver clasped his long knobby fingers together across his concave belly. "She's worked so hard all these years, raising you alone after that crazy jackass of a kid of mine ran off. And trying to keep me healthy to boot."

"My father," Alison said with a frown, "wasn't crazy . . . or a jackass either, for that matter. Maybe if you'd tried just once to talk with him . . . but you're both so stubborn."

She paused to swallow hard, as she always seemed to have to do when she spoke of her father. She'd been defending him all the time, especially to her mother, since he'd suddenly started writing to her from Rockport, about a year ago. He never actually explained to her why he'd left when she was a baby. Nor did he apologize exactly. But she treasured his letters. They showed a keen and uncritical interest in her — Alison O'Brien, young woman and budding artist.

"And," she continued, "don't give me that junk about your being a burden. You were a big help to Mom. Especially with me."

"Maybe so. For a while. But then this damn Parkinson's disease . . . the tremors and such. Lord, how I've aged the last few years."

Alison glanced at his hands. He was trying to hold them still in his lap, but she could detect some shaking. She could almost feel it in her own hands as a tingling, hear it as a high-pitched tremolo.

The medication that Oliver had been taking for several months had dramatically improved his overall condition — the rigidity of his muscles, the slowness, even the depression, the sitting around. ("Waiting to die," he'd commented once, in the worst of it, as if he'd just said he was waiting for the bus. Alison had gone cold all over.)

But some of the shaking lingered on. A resting tremor, they called it, most noticeable when he was still. "I can get a glass of juice to my mouth without so much as a wobble," he'd say, "but try to stop long enough to drink the damn stuff, and oops, here we go again. Get the spot remover."

Alison had devised a way to keep him moving to fight the hated tremors and the depression at the same time. She'd put a certain record on — Enesco's first Rumanian Rhapsody. That piece, he'd always said, could set even his teeth to dancing. There was simply no way to sit through it in stillness. It usually worked, too. Got him out of his sagging armchair, uplifted his sagging spirit. Many late afternoons passed *presto*, Oliver conducting and Alison being the orchestra, or they'd switch roles. Oliver did an especially good Gypsy violin.

They hadn't needed Enesco as much lately. "I'm good as new," he claimed. Alison had thought so too. Until the strangeness began. But if Oliver was acting a little bizarre sometimes, it was because her mother didn't believe in his recovery enough. Self-fulfilling prophecies. Alison had read about such things. Senility brought on by uncaring families who thought that's how old people were supposed to act.

". . . finally putting together a life for herself," Oliver was saying and Alison wasn't sure what she'd missed. "With friends, a good job at the bank, even some dates. She deserves all that."

"I wish you wouldn't always defend my mother. Even back when she didn't believe you were really sick, still you —"

"Wait a minute. What do you mean, she didn't believe I was sick?"

"You know. Back when your Parkinson's symptoms came and went. It was weird. One minute you could hardly get up from a chair or take a step, like your foot was glued, you said. And then suddenly you were as strong as an ox, and quick too. Remember when you jumped up to catch that stack of dishes I'd left on the table, too close to the edge? Two seconds earlier, you'd been —"

"I know, I know. But I didn't realize . . . she didn't believe I was sick? She thought I was faking it?"

Alison sighed. They should have gotten back on the road ages ago, she thought. Why were they sitting here like this? Maybe she was even more frightened than she'd thought. "No, of course she didn't think you were faking it."

"Nuts, then. Losing my marbles. Turning into an old codger."

Alison didn't answer. He never used to be so touchy, she was sure. "The point I was trying to make is that you always defend her, even though she's the one who wants to send you away. And she *would* have, too. 'He shouldn't be left alone.' She's said it a million times."

"What started all that up again? I've been meaning to ask you. As good as I've been feeling, it doesn't make much sense to me. Unless . . ." His voice had the childish sound of someone who does not really want an answer.

Alison pretended to be busy examining the map.

"I suppose I've been a little absent-minded lately." He continued. "A little . . . well, flighty perhaps? No, that's not it."

She felt his eyes on her again, searching her face. "We'll stop for lunch after we get past Madison," she said. "Okay?"

He did not answer and she shifted uneasily in her seat.

"Ready to go?" She glanced at him.

He seemed to be checking out the back seat for something important.

"What do you need?"

There was something creeping into his mood that she wanted him to shrug off as quickly as possible.

"Want your recorder or something? Here, I'll get it." She pushed up on her legs and arched her back to grab for his recorder in the back seat.

"Don't!"

His voice startled her, and she froze in an awkward leaning-back position. Her legs began to tremble a little, and she reached back farther. "I just want — "

He gave her arm a sudden swat, forcing her away from the back seat.

She was too stunned to say anything. Her forearm smarted, but worse than that, she felt his inexplicable anger like a steel door slammed against her.

His hands began kneading the sides of his face. "I knew they'd come," he groaned. "It's just not that easy to run away, is it?"

"Oliver." Alison steadied herself against the steering wheel. "What are you talking about? Don't do this."

He lifted his face from the shadows of his hands. "I'm sorry, honey. Forgive me. It's . . . it's nothing."

She turned the key, jerked the car into drive, and drove back onto the highway, back on course. *Nothing*. Like hell it was nothing. She'd been sure he would be fine once she had him all to herself, away from everything.

It was always so sudden and terrifying. The look on his face — eerie, unseeing. The first time she'd noticed something wrong had been two weeks before, when she'd come home from school to find his door closed.

There'd been this daily ritual between them for years. She would come into his room after school and drop something into his eager hands, usually her own artwork, or sometimes big, glossy books of art. He would examine her work solemnly, nodding, criticizing, but not unkindly. They would talk about other artists, discussing their styles, sometimes arguing, often laughing. It was a time of day they'd always shared.

But when he started closing his door to her she was left

with all that empty time, and the treasures she was used to sharing with him weighed heavy in her hands, with no place to put them. She listened at his door a few times before going on to her own room and tossing her things into a corner. Twice she slammed her door meaningfully, but still his door was closed until dinner.

The rest of the time he seemed completely normal. So much better than before, when his face had settled into a fixed, withdrawn expression, almost masklike, and when his hands had shaken much worse, and he'd walked as if about to topple forward at any moment.

When she'd listened at his door one day, heard the talking and laughter, the jostling into furniture, she could bear it no longer. Without knocking, she'd barged in. There he'd stood — hands in midgesture, feet apart, his mouth open. He'd been talking to someone and there was no one in sight. After a moment, she had closed the door again, embarrassed and frightened.

He sat, now, subdued but apparently alert. "Wisconsin Dels," he said. "I brought your dad here once when he was a tyke. Or . . ." He rubbed his cheek again. "Was it that I meant to . . . once."

She needed him to laugh. She searched her mind frantically for a joke. Then she saw the billboard ahead. "Hey — look at that! They must really grow birds big out here."

"What? Where?"

"Right there. Says: 'Ride the original Wisconsin Dels Ducks.' They must be some ducks, big as ponies, huh?"

Oliver stared at her for a moment. "They aren't *duck* ducks; they're these amphibious contraptions — "

"I know that. I know," she shouted. "God, where's your sense of humor?"

He shook his head as if to jostle some loose pieces back

into place. "Sorry," he said. "I don't know what gets into me lately. I just don't know."

Alison sighed. "I'm sorry too. I didn't mean to shout at you."

They drove in silence for several hours and, while she fought off the hypnotic effects of the highway, he drifted into a nap. "Lucky duck," she whispered, then smiled to herself and barely resisted nudging him. "Ducks, get it?"

Chapter 3

"WHERE ARE WE?" Oliver asked.

"It's time to stop," Alison declared. "I'm going berserk and we need gas. Are you as hungry as I am?"

"Hungrier. Where are we?" he repeated, looking around with squinted eyes.

"Past Madison. We'll eat lunch at this truck stop."

"You're the boss," he said, stretching his arms and legs as far as the compact car would allow. "Damn leg fell asleep."

"Watch your language," she said. "I'm such an impressionable young thing."

"Like hell," he said as he pounded on his leg with a fist.

They both limped to the truck stop, Alison sniffing at the french-fry smell and trying to work up an appetite for overused grease.

The restaurant was small and unpretentious. The primary color was gray, but it was a cool, clean kind of gray that Alison welcomed. Bright green menus, stuck into metal holders, had the effect of evergreen trees in winter.

There were three heavyset truck drivers lined up at the counter, perched on barstools too small for them. A pretty waitress chatted with them as she sucked delicately on a cigarette. The tables were empty, except one where a young man in a business suit was sipping coffee and drumming his fingertips on a large untidy pile of papers. Oliver, as Alison expected, chose a table near the businessman and tossed him a grin. The man nodded and then glanced out the window at his side.

"Look at that young fellow over there," Oliver whispered.

Alison didn't have to look at him. "What about him?"

"He's a peddler. I can spot 'em a mile away."

She rolled her eyes. Here it comes, she thought.

Oliver scanned the menu placed before him but kept glancing at the other man. Finally he cleared his throat. "Looks like you got a mess of paperwork there. Call reports?"

The man nodded again, his skin flushing as he tried to straighten up the papers on his table. "I hate this part of the job," he said, and then looked at Oliver nervously, perhaps wondering if he was some kind of informer.

"Don't blame you," Oliver said.

"I've been at this for months now, and I just get worse and worse at filling in all the blanks so I don't get yelled at."

"What're you selling?"

"Hardware. Mostly hand tools." He laughed, holding up a thumb. "Nearly chopped this right off first day out. Maybe if I had, the guy would have felt sorry enough for me to buy my stuff."

Oliver laughed and shook his head. "Me, I was an insurance man, but, believe me, the rejection feels the same. And the drowning in paperwork too."

The young man nodded and glared at the pile of paperwork as he sipped his coffee. His hands were much too large for him and Alison wondered if the excessive weight of them was responsible for his sloping shoulders. He seemed to be searching for his next remark.

"Details," Oliver continued. "Heaven forbid you should hold up a sale by leaving some meaningless blank — "

"Oliver, please," Alison said and gestured toward the waitress approaching on spongy-soled shoes. She was taking her time to perfect her walk for the attentive truck drivers.

"Figure out what you want to order," Alison whispered. "We haven't got all day to sit and chin with strangers." She was not always aware when she used one of Oliver's expressions, but this time she did it on purpose. "Chinning" described him perfectly when he went into one of his "I'm just an old peddler" routines.

Oliver looked up at the blond waitress. "We'll have a cheeseburger, fries, and strawberry malt each, if you please," he told her with the kind of wink that always made Alison blush.

"I didn't order that," she said, glancing at the waitress who stopped her writing. Alison noticed that she had just applied plum-colored lipstick. If her teeth were tobacco-stained, as Alison suspected, they were well hidden. Smiling appeared to be reserved for customers who looked like better tippers.

"That's the lunch you want, isn't it?" Oliver asked.

"Well, yes, but — "

"And make it snappy, miss," he said. "We haven't got all day, according to my granddaughter here."

After the waitress bustled off, he turned back to the salesman. "Got any Abe Lincolns in that pile of call reports?"

The young man cocked one of his dark eyebrows. "Beg your pardon?"

Oliver laughed again, winking at Alison as if she would

know what he was talking about (which she did not). "Abe Lincolns. Coined the phrase myself and all my friends picked it up, but I suppose you'd never . . . anyway, they're fake customers."

The salesman uncocked his eyebrow and blinked several times. He was beginning to look annoyed, Alison thought, but she was never sure about the way people reacted to Oliver.

"You gotta see x number of people, right?" Oliver asked. "So if you run out of time or just plain wear out, you make some up. Fill in the blanks any which way. It used to work for me. At least it did until I started getting too cocky." He looked at Alison. "My favorites, by the way, were names like Peter Rubens and Al Dürer."

Alison widened her eyes and gasped.

"Sure, *you* know who they are, being such an art buff. But most people aren't hard to fool. Until I got stupid one day and wrote up a call report on a fellow named Vincent Vango, spelled V-A-N-G-O, mind you. And in his medical history I listed an amputated ear."

Alison giggled and the young salesman cupped his mouth with his long fingers.

"Well," Oliver said, "needless to say, I had to play it straight for a while after that."

The salesman gave a hearty, appreciative laugh, and then, glancing at his watch, he stuffed his papers into a fancy briefcase so new Alison could smell the leather from where she sat. "It's been nice chatting with you, sir," he said. "But I gotta go if I ever plan to get home tomorrow." He sighed and rubbed the back of his neck. "I do miss being home, you know?"

"Ah, yes. It's tough," Oliver said with a sympathetic grimace. "Figuring out what comes first — family or work —

and how to be a halfway decent husband and father when you *are* home. Right, son?"

"Right . . ." The man began edging off his chair, clearly waiting for the best moment to stand up.

But Oliver was preparing to give him the full treatment. "Being a parent is tough at the best of times," he continued, leaning back in his chair, looking as if he'd light up a pipe if he had one. "But when your work takes you away from the family more than the average Joe who puts in his eight hours, well, I'll tell you, you have to be quite a juggler, an acrobat . . . a whole damn circus act." He looked to Alison for a reaction, but she only smiled weakly and waited for the young man to leave.

"Oh, you have to work hard, sure," Oliver said. "You have to provide. But it's the excess that gets dangerous, you know what I mean?"

The young man shook his head and then nodded, his legs still poised to stand up. His expression indicated to Alison that he thought her grandfather was some kind of weirdo. Feeling sympathy for Oliver, who was still talking, she turned her gaze back to him.

". . . she'd say to me, and she was right, absolutely. I enjoyed being overworked, dog-tired, hanging from the edge by my fingernails. Crazy as that sounds. Addiction to excess — I'm not sure if I heard that somewhere or made it up. But anyway, by the time I'd mellowed, it was too late. My wife had learned to rely on . . . everyone *but* me. My son had learned not to need me anymore. Not one bit." Oliver hesitated, pulled forward a bit. "Strangers," he muttered. "You end up in a house full of strangers."

The man coughed and slowly stood up. "Well, take it easy," he said before making his escape.

"Hey." Alison grabbed Oliver's arm and jerked it. "Let's

plan our trip." She didn't like the film coming over his eyes and the frown dragging down his face, although she told herself it was just another one of his ramblings that carried him where he didn't want to go. "You're my navigator. Let's take a look at the maps and plan our stops. I wonder how long it will take us to get there."

She made a lot of commotion spreading maps and tourbooks in front of Oliver's distracted face. But then their lunches arrived and Alison stuck everything back onto the seat for the moment. Oliver ate silently.

"It's funny," Alison said, mostly to fill the silence, "but I never knew you cheated like that, Oliver."

He gave her a sharp, startled look. "What? I never . . . Who said I cheated?"

Alison felt her food lump together halfway down to her stomach. "You did. Just now. You know, your Abe Lincolns?"

He let out his breath. "Oh . . . that. No, I suppose I never mentioned that before."

After another long silence, he finally pushed away his plate and stared at Alison. "What exactly is it you want from him, anyway?"

"From who?"

"From my . . . from your father. Going all the way to Rockport, you . . . you . . . might be expecting too much."

"After what you just said to that salesman, how can you even ask?" She could tell immediately she shouldn't have reminded him. He needed, she thought, to have lighter thoughts. Maybe even to laugh at something. Anything. "It all started when I found out (with no help from you, by the way) that there was a man involved in making me. I think I used to have some juvenile notion of a miraculous conception, you know?"

Oliver grinned then and they both relaxed, shoving down their congealing cheeseburgers, and then lingering over their malts. She finished hers first. "He's my father, that's all," she said quietly. "Maybe I'm obsessed; I don't know. I think I used to be. That word, *father*, always seemed to me so . . . so important. I'd hear things like 'father of our country' and 'God the Father.' And . . . and when have you ever heard of a founding mother?"

"Feminist mumbo jumbo. You sound like your mother."

"Oliver! How can you say that? That's not the point. I'm talking about how I grew up feeling something . . . missing, you know? I needed to get *his* side of things. I needed to see Mom once in a while through *his* eyes. And hear about how they met and fell in love and stuff from him. Even to hear their fights for myself, not from you fifteen years later. You and Mom only seem to remember the bad parts. Sometimes I wonder if she ever loved him at all. If *anyone* did."

Oliver was having trouble looking at her. After a pause, he nodded and then got up to go to the rest room.

Alison watched him walk away from her and closed her eyes, wishing she could tell him what it was like, so he'd understand and not get hurt. Living with her father's disappearance was like a small death within her. In her blackest moods, she wished it could be a bigger death, a real one. Then, at least, she could stop lying about her father.

Why wasn't it possible to get through childhood without constant prickly reminders of fathers? Teachers chirping: "Tell your mothers and fathers . . ." and "Where does *your* father work?" Banquets that were cruelly tagged "Father/ Daughter Night." She'd imagined them in great detail — frilly-dressed girls blushing as their doting fathers guided them across polished dance floors. (Oliver had really been hurt when she hadn't told him about the dance in time for him to take her.)

Even those other kids, whose parents were divorced, usually got to see their fathers, sometimes for grand, adventurous weekends or summer vacations.

Her official story now was that her dad was in Europe, and that was only in those rare instances when she could talk about him at all. "In Europe. Studying art. With some guy named Giovanni something-or-other. Studying the masters." He really had done that once, long ago. It wasn't such an outrageous lie. "He's very caught up in his work. But I get these great postcards . . ."

What a laugh. Sometimes she could laugh about it. With her friend Molly. For some reason she could talk to her about what really happened with her father. And for those moments she'd feel better. Molly was the greatest listener Alison had ever known. And the greatest laugher. A soft, fair type. Blond fluff on her head, scarcely any eyebrows at all. Dark brown eyes stuck, as if by mistake, in the palest skin, like raisins in unbaked cookies.

There was another reason Alison liked being at Molly's house. She had the sort of father Alison dreamed of. He was tall, with a broad lap that was always ready for both girls when they'd been younger. And, more recently, he'd started teasing Alison in an almost grown-up, flirtatious way. Calling her "K-K-K-Katy" because he said she was growing up into a Hepburn type.

Sometimes Molly seemed a little jealous, and maybe that was partly why she was the one to come up with the idea of driving to Rockport. Alison wondered now, facing up to the potential pain, if that had been Molly's way of saying "find your own dad." But no, that couldn't be.

"Are we going to make a day of it, here in this scenic

spot?" Oliver's voice came from above her head and she opened her eyes. "Time to move on."

"I was just resting my aching eyes."

Oliver grunted but in a sympathetic way.

"Oliver?"

"What?"

"Maybe we should turn around and go back."

He looked at her as though she'd just vomited her lunch at his feet. "What are you talking about?" He returned to his spot opposite her in the booth.

"I was just thinking out loud. Maybe this is a mistake." She was surprised at how distressed he looked. Hadn't he been trying to talk her out of the trip just a few minutes ago? "You're the one who said I'm probably expecting too much of Dad."

"Did I say that?"

Sitting across from him in the booth, she found it difficult to avoid Oliver's melancholy, liquidy eyes. When he started sorting through the bottles of pills from his pocket, Alison's alarm tightened in her chest. He wasn't due for his Parkinson's medicine again. "What's wrong, Oliver? Don't you feel well?"

"I'm fine," he replied. "Just need another one of my sneeze pills is all."

"Oh. If you're sure that's all."

"This has always been the worst time of year for me, you know."

"I don't hear you humming."

"I don't like making a complete fool of myself."

"Oh?" She widened her eyes. "Since when?"

"Stop joking around," he scolded.

She found the pills and deposited two in his hand, but he only stared at them, shaking his head.

31

"What's the matter now?" she asked.

"Nothing. Just waiting for you to make up your mind, that's all."

"If I can't talk to you about my doubts, then who can I talk to?"

"Thatta girl. Keep talking."

"Well, you're a big help. What do *you* think we should do? Tell me."

He popped the pills into his mouth and grimaced before washing them down with water and then with the pink milky remains of his malt. "I'll go along with whatever you and your mother decide."

Alison felt her face heat up. "I'm not going to lose you too. Not because of her or anybody else."

Oliver's eyes moistened even more. Had he caught the pills in his throat? She didn't want to think he was about to cry. Not Oliver. He hadn't even cried when they'd told him he had Parkinson's disease, an old person's disease that would probably play a role in his eventual death. In fact, she thought she remembered him trying to laugh it off and cheer her up, but maybe her memory was playing tricks on her. The same kind of tricks Oliver's memory had always played on him – making him tell a story a little differently, a little better each time. She did a lot of things like he did.

"Hey, Gramps," she said gently, coaxing him back to himself. "Let's forget about this whole stupid lunch. We're together, aren't we? We're doing the right thing – going to Rockport? It's some kind of action at least. Right?"

"Maybe we should call your father, so he'll be sure to be there. What if he – "

"He'll be there. His last letter mentioned an art show he was participating in – from June fourth to the tenth, in Rockport. He'll be there; don't worry."

He nodded. "We have to call your mother, though. Soon."

"Sure, sure. Can't wait to get yelled at again."

"Didn't used to be this way between you two," he remarked casually, getting up to leave.

"I know that. Don't you think I know that?" She stood up and dug out some money from her bag.

"I always thought you two were about as close as a mother and daughter can be," he said.

She paid their bill and followed him outside. The solid warm breeze blew something into her eye. "So did I," she said. "So did I."

Chapter 4

"*H*ERE." SHE TOSSED the Triptik at him. "Before we go any further, we better study this thing, figure out where we're going to stay tonight.

"Camp out?"

"Better make it a motel tonight. I'm going to need a good sleep. It might rain or something." There was not a cloud in sight, but he didn't question her reasoning. Whenever they'd camped out before – usually in their backyard – it had always been Alison who complained the next morning and gave in to the luxuries of soft beds, running water, and electricity. But he never teased her about being spoiled or soft. Not once.

They leaned against the car and used the hood like a table, spreading out maps and books that they didn't even need yet. Figuring about where they'd be at 7:00 each night, they planned to go to bed right after supper and get up and be on the road the next day as early as possible. At that rate, they'd be in Rockport in four days. Oliver gathered the maps, put them away, and gave her a brisk salute.

"And no more long lunches like this one," she said, returning his salute.

"Right, Chief."

Before opening her door, Alison pulled up the sticky waistband of her jeans and pulled down her shirt. She watched the way the shirt flattened her breasts to nothing if she tugged hard enough on it, until she felt her grandfather's eyes boring into her chest too.

"They still lopsided?" he asked.

"What? Oh . . . Oliver. We shouldn't be discussing things like that anymore, now that I'm a woman."

"Whatever you say, miss." Oliver chuckled as he got into the car.

Alison felt her stomach wringing itself out. Her grandfather had been the only one last year to whom she could confide that one of her breasts was growing much faster than the other. And he hadn't known what to say, besides "Ask your mother about it." But Alison had expected her mother to notice the problem herself and offer advice. She would have, Alison was sure, if she hadn't been so busy.

"Want me to drive?" Oliver asked when Alison started the car.

"I thought you didn't have a license."

"I'm not sure. Maybe it's still valid. Let me drive for a couple of hours. You look terrible."

"Thanks a lot," Alison grumbled, but she was grateful when they exchanged seats.

The talk about drivers' licenses made her edgy. She started to sweat every time she saw a police car, even those going in the opposite direction. Once, a patrol car followed them for several miles. Oliver seemed unalarmed, his foot just as heavy on the accelerator, his steering just as erratic.

"Slow down," she whispered.

"I'm going fifty-five," he said, "and why are you whispering?" He swerved to the right as he turned to speak to her.

Her hand jerked out automatically toward the wheel, her foot stomped an imaginary brake on her side.

"What's the matter with you, Chief?"

"That cop car behind us. Maybe somehow he knows."

"Knows what?"

"That it's us," she answered.

Oliver shook his head. "Get some sleep. . . . Look, he just exited. Your cop doesn't want us at all. He's after bigger fish."

Alison tried to sleep, but her eyelids alternately clenched and drifted open. Just as a dream would start to creep in, a large bump in the road or a car honking and Oliver's swerving would shove her forehead into the window at her side. Licking her lips and clearing away gravel from her throat, she tried again, and again.

She wanted to dream about some tall, dark stranger who would enter her messy life and clear away the rubble. But the stranger kept taking on Jordan's broad features, no matter how she resisted. Jordan would be, she figured, about the perfect boyfriend, if only she could talk to him about her mother. Those two — Jordan and her mother — were just too cozy to suit her. She recalled the line from some old Laurel and Hardy movie, from back when she and her mother used to watch them together: "Like two peas in a pod."

Laurel and Hardy movies had been very special to Alison and her mother. They had usually been on TV in the middle of the night. The two of them would get up and make popcorn at 2 A.M. Then they'd watch the movie, their two pairs of icy feet tucked into the same blanket at opposite ends. Trying in vain to stifle their laughter so Oliver would not be disturbed, they'd gleefully anticipate the next line, and the next, in unison. "Like two peas in a pod."

But Laurel and Hardy weren't on TV much anymore. So one night Jordan had brought over his new VCR and had rented two of their best films, as requested by Alison's mother.

"Jordan's never seen them," her mother explained to Alison. "He's had such a deprived childhood."

Alison watched Jordan's muscular back as he hooked up the machine to their old TV. "Maybe he won't think they're that great, Mom. Don't be disappointed and bitchy if—"

"Of course he will," her mother said.

And of course he did. He and her mother both had a fit watching the movies. When Laurel and Hardy did their irresistible little dance in front of the saloon in *Way Out West*, Jordan had actually started kicking up his thick soccer-player legs along with them. And her mother clapped and giggled like a girl.

Alison tried to concentrate on the screen and, for once, saw only a fat man and a skinny man in outrageously baggy pants, making fools of themselves. She felt robbed of some favorite possession.

During *Blockheads*, Jordan sat leaning forward. "I don't believe this stuff," he said about the misadventures on the endless flights of stairs. "This is some of the most inventive comedy I've ever seen." His gray eyes darted from Alison to her mother. His smile was so inviting, but she didn't know who it was meant for — her or her mother. "Genius," he said. "Sheer genius."

Her mother sat there beaming as if she, single-handedly, had been responsible for the comedy team's genius.

Alison stood up, fearing she'd scream at her mother if she didn't do something else. "Popcorn," she announced. "I'll make popcorn."

"I'll help." Jordan started to get up from the couch he shared with Alison.

"Not now." Alison's mother said. "This is one of the best scenes. Wait."

"We can always rewind it," Jordan said, pausing only a moment before following Alison into the kitchen.

Over the roar of the air popper, they could hear Alison's mother, still laughing in the living room.

"Your mom's funny," Jordan said as he put some butter on the stove to melt.

"Funny ha ha or funny peculiar?"

Jordan only grinned at her.

"You don't *have* to like Laurel and Hardy, you know. My mom gets carried away sometimes. We used to watch those old movies, Mom and I, late at night. She'd actually wake me up to watch them with her. I'd be exhausted the next day. Kind of weird, huh?"

"Depends on how you look at it. *My* mom still likes to tuck me in for ten hours of sleep a night. Like I was four years old or something. As long as I've got younger brothers, I have to follow *their* rules. Drives me nuts."

Alison found the popcorn salt and then watched the popping kernels jump into the bowl. "How about your dad? Does he treat you like a kid too?"

"My dad? No, he's the opposite."

"What do you mean?"

"Well, like last week when he took me aside for one of his 'Son, it's time we talked' discussions. He told me I should start learning how to invest my money wisely. Can you believe it? I've got all of two hundred and thirty-six dollars saved but he acts as though it was twenty grand. So he starts in about annuities and certificates and stuff, and I said, 'Actually, I was looking forward to the new racetrack opening so I could get a *real* fast return on my money.' "

Alison unplugged the popper and shook the popcorn bowl to distribute butter and salt. "You mean you want to gamble?"

"Of course not. I was joking. JOKING. But he gives me this special nod of his and the great I-understand-you-son look. Of course, I know he's dying of worry inside, so to make him feel better I enrolled in a class at the Y about investments. The most gruesome hours I've ever had to sit through. Incredible, my old man is."

Alison laughed. "Sometimes it *is* hard to tell when you're serious."

Jordan took the bowl from her hands and set it back on the counter. "Serious?" He pushed some stray hairs from her face and seemed to be studying it. "I can be. In fact, I'm getting more serious all the time."

"Hey kids!" Alison's mom shouted from the living room. "Where's that popcorn? And how do you rewind this dumb thing?"

Later, after Jordan had left, giving Alison a quick, sweet kiss outside the door, Alison and her mother had fought.

"Well," her mother said, "did you and Jordan have fun out there?"

"I'd rather not talk about it, if you don't mind."

"Oh come on. Give your old mom a thrill."

"Stop trying to be funny, Mom. It's gross."

"Now why would I be trying to be funny, with a daughter who's been sparkling with such good humor all evening? What's your problem anyway? You want me to be involved in your life and when I am, you jump all over me."

"I didn't think men were exactly your cup of tea, that's all. Why pick on Jordan?"

Her mother smiled. "Pick on? Don't be ridiculous. I'm interested in him, sure. For *you*."

"Well, I can be interested in someone for myself, thanks."

"I'm not so sure of that. He's not like other boys and you don't seem to appreciate that."

"What do you mean, not like other boys?"

"He's not as likely to . . . to hurt you, I don't think."

"You mean all men are monsters," Alison said. "All except Jordan. Well, maybe I happen to like monsters."

Her mother apparently chose to ignore that remark, which, as always, made Alison want to bite back her own words and spit them out again in much better form.

"What are you growling about?" It was Oliver's voice coming from some distance away.

Alison opened her eyes, tight against the inside of the window of the moving car.

"Are you carsick or something?"

She straightened up in her seat and rotated her stiff neck. "No. I'm okay."

"You were growling, though. No doubt about that."

"So, some people talk in their sleep, I growl."

"Sorry I mentioned it."

"I was thinking about Mom."

"Well, that explains it."

"Oliver, do you think she hates men? In general, I mean."

He looked startled. "Hates men?"

"Yes," Alison said.

He rubbed the side of his nose. "I wouldn't say she hates men. Not exactly. Mistrusts might be a better word."

"Well, whatever you call it, I wonder if I'm getting to be the same way. Maybe even worse. You know very well how a kid tries to be like her mother. I could turn into one of those women who spends most of her life fighting men."

"I wasn't aware there was such a group." Oliver smiled infuriatingly.

"Sure there is. I've read about them. Seen a few too. They walk around ready to kick a man where it hurts for no reason at all. Just because he's a man."

"Alison, for heaven's sake. Where do you come up with such nonsense?"

"You're still back in the Middle Ages; that's your problem."

"I count on you to keep me enlightened," he said.

"What about all that time Mom spent tracking down a woman neurologist for you? No one else would do."

"She picked the best doctor. It's as simple as that."

Alison ignored him. "She scares away every man she dates."

"She likes Jordan."

Alison found she wanted to growl again. "She's not dating Jordan. *I* am."

"I only meant —"

"This new guy she met, Richard, he won't be around long either — just you wait. I've seen her in action, with her 'let's get things straight right from the start' attitude."

"Your mother is not one to compromise much, that's for sure. Not anymore." Oliver smiled sadly, something clearly draining pleasure from his memory.

They were silent for several miles. Alison wished she would stop thinking about her mother. But so many questions seemed to be nudging her, now that her mother was miles away.

"Mom was pretty young when she had me, I guess," Alison said matter-of-factly.

"She's still young. Not quite thirty-five yet."

Alison looked at Oliver in a way that she knew he'd take as permission to carry on about her mother if he wished.

"I always figured that's why you two were so close — she was such a kid herself. But with grown-up problems and responsibilities. I was so glad to have the two of you stay on with me after your dad took off. You were just tiny yet, still screaming half the night, which you did, incidentally, much more than was reasonable. She had no money. Well, that was why the three of you had moved in with me in the first place. Her folks had turned their backs . . . never could figure that one out."

He started wandering into the next lane until the sharp yelp of a horn straightened him out again. Alison closed her eyes.

"Anyway," Oliver continued, "she needed me more than ever after Gerard left, that was for sure. And I was ready to slow down at work. Semiretired, they called it. Still taking in renewal checks and taking care of a few old clients — my 'cream' I called them, the way they separated and rose to the top. Besides, I'd been stashing some money away ever since your grandma died. So I was able to help and I wanted to . . . more than she ever knew."

Alison leaned back. She'd heard most of this before, but every now and then, her grandfather would stick something new in like a fresh batch of cookies tossed in with the old, crumbly ones.

"Your mom, when I first met her, was, well, I can still see her. Lovely Tess. Such a quiet girl, long hair parted in the middle and held down by an Indian band — that was before it was so fashionable, mind you. Midsixties."

"She still wore her hair that way when I was born," Alison said. "I've seen the pictures."

"And nuts about the Beatles. She used to recite the words of their songs to me. Trying to convert me, I think, but I was a hopeless Lawrence Welk fan. She was going to study philosophy, she told me, at some Eastern girls' college. I forget which one. Had a scholarship lined up. Until she, well . . . it's funny, but I think it was her individuality, her style that Gerard fell in love with." Oliver snorted. "And then he was so damn surprised and disillusioned when he couldn't turn her into a housewife and mother and secretary and bookkeeper and leaning post all at once."

Alison listened intently. She'd never heard about the plans to study philosophy. Closing her eyes, she tried to imagine seeing her mother, eighteen years younger, walking across a plush green New England campus, school books tucked across her chest, red hair swinging loose from the leather band at the top like unwoven fleece. Carrying her obsession with the Beatles like a shield against everydayness.

"She had to go back to work right after you were born, of course, to support him," Oliver continued. "All Gerard knew was painting, and he hadn't even finished school yet. I tried to stay out of their lives even though I was mad as hell at the two of them. They were always bickering about something, usually money. And about failure. 'Stop leaning on me,' Tess would say. 'Grow up.' And then Gerard would pipe in with his complaints that other artists had nice strong supportive wives.

"She knew what she was getting into when she married him," Alison commented. "Or she should have. If she appreciated his talent at all, she should have been willing to —"

"Willing to what? Give up on her own talents?"

Alison shrugged.

"You artists are all alike, you know that? Think you

have the corner on greatness. Well, there are other things in life that are just as important. Other dreams."

Alison felt injured. "All I know is that they should have been able to work things out."

"Ah, but that's assuming plenty of time to get to know each other and to . . . well, mature. Those hurry-up weddings bring on their own special problems."

Alison blinked and leaned forward a little to see his face.

He was wincing and shaking his head. "Damn. I always knew I'd do that someday."

"They had to get married?"

He shook his head again.

"They had to?" she repeated.

"You weren't supposed to know. I don't understand why not, but that's what Tess — "

"They got married because Mom was pregnant? With me? That doesn't make sense. I was born in nineteen sixty-eight. Mom always told me they were married in nineteen sixty-six."

He was still shaking his head. "She had a . . . a stillborn baby first time. It was . . .'" Oliver seemed to be examining an old pain, poking at it to see if it could still hurt so bad.

"Stillborn?" Alison's voice came out harsh, squawkish. "A dead baby?" She shuddered. Tiny blue fingers and toes, matted-down hair — what color? Red, like her mother's? Brown, like Alison's? Then another thought, even more painful. The ache of tears traveled across the bridge of her nose, stabbed her eye sockets. "Girl or boy?" she asked quietly.

"Girl," he answered. His right hand left the wheel to seek out her arm and give it a few not too gentle pats. Then the hand returned eagerly, gratefully perhaps, to the task of driving.

44

"You'd think – " Alison swallowed. "She might have told me."

"Now wait a minute," Oliver said. "The last thing I want to do is make it worse between you two. She's had a tough time of it, Alison. Try to be a 'woman' like you claim to be and put yourself in her place for once. She's never mentioned that baby to anyone. Ever."

Alison lifted her legs to curl up tightly into a ball. She pressed her knees hard into her eyes until she saw blue and white sparks behind her lids. Her breath was warm on her legs. "I always wanted a sister," she said at last.

"And your mother," Oliver said, "always wanted a large family."

For the moment there was nothing more to say.

Chapter 5

THE MIDAFTERNOON sun felt fiery on the back of Alison's head. She reached up to touch her hair and thought she heard it crackle. The car was stopped.

"It's so hot," she mumbled and discovered some drool below the right corner of her mouth. "Was I really asleep?"

"You bet. Feel better?"

"I feel like I died. I didn't even dream. Nothing. Just a chunk of time gone. How long?"

He shrugged. "Not very, I'm afraid."

She sat up and looked around. They were parked at a Howard Johnson's that sat above the thruway. She glanced at the Triptik by his side; it had not been flipped. The top half of the shaded block that was Chicago sat at the bottom of the page, an awesome tip of an iceberg.

"This is an oasis," Oliver said. "Last one, I think, before the city. I had to stop."

"It's okay, Oliver. There's no problem."

"I don't know about that. There might be. I think I missed where I was supposed to turn off to bypass Chicago. I should have woken you up. I kept thinking you'd wake up by yourself when I had to stop for tollbooths. They started as soon as we entered Illinois. But you were sleeping so soundly, I didn't have the heart . . ."

"Oliver. I'm awake now. What were you saying about missing the bypass?"

"All of a sudden the farm country seemed to give way to suburbs, but there weren't many signs saying how far away Chicago was. The air looked different and traffic picked up, and then I started seeing the signs for Route two ninety-four, where I was supposed to turn off. But I think I missed it somehow. Just before this oasis I saw a sign with an arrow going off to the right and I'm sure it said two ninety-something. But it was too late for me to turn. Now we're on our way into the city. We'll get lost for sure."

Alison banged the heel of her hand onto her head to clear her thinking. "I don't think we're lost, Oliver. We'll ask inside. Come on." They climbed out of the car. From some corner of her muddled mind came the reminder: "Your medicine, Oliver."

"Already got it out. I'm overdue again. The doctor would kill me."

"Yes, she would," Allison added. "The old bat."

They entered the large glass building that sat like a bridge over the traffic. It was nearly empty. Alison was reminded of movie theaters; it had the same popcorn smell and soft red carpet. They stood in line for Cokes and asked the cashier about Route 294. In broken English, he assured them that 294 was ahead of them, not behind. Oliver looked unconvinced and kept asking loud, childish questions until Alison urged him toward a table.

"Stop worrying," she said. "We're fine. I'll drive now so you can rest. Boy, you're right about the scenery and air changing quickly. Tollbooths already, huh?"

Oliver nodded.

"You know what I hate most about driving?" she asked him. "It's not being able to look at things. Really look. It kills me."

He nodded again. "It was beautiful all right. Those rock formations back in Wisconsin, right at the edge of the highway."

"I wonder if anyone climbs those," she said. "The view must be something from up there."

"Too steep."

Alison looked out the window and recalled, just after lunch, looking past one of the large red barns, its roof freckled with birds, into a crown of pine trees. It had seemed like an offering; the sun and her imagination had supplied the jewels. "I could feel my fingers twitch," she said. "For my pencils. But there we were, stuck to the highway like a train to a track."

"Maybe we should try for more rest stops," he said.

"Maybe."

They finished their Cokes and found the rest rooms. Inside the ladies' room was a family of small children, difficult to count because of their constant, frenetic activity. The mother stood in a corner marked for babies, changing a diaper on her youngest and periodically rearranging her limp dress.

When Alison started to leave, so did the family, and she found herself swept into a tidepool of squeals and pasty limbs bouncing off each other. They found their exhausted-looking father waiting near Oliver, outside the bathroom door. Oliver backed away as if under attack when he saw the children. The noise dispersed quickly into the still, open space outside, but Oliver's alarm appeared to remain.

He crept closer to Alison and said, out of the corner of his mouth, "Let's get away from here."

"They're just a little out of control, after being cooped up so long," she reassured him. "That one over there is a real cutie, don't you think?"

But Oliver rushed to the car, pale and tight-faced.

He must be awfully tired, she thought, if he doesn't want to chat with those people. "Hey, Oliver, did you find out what the guy does for a living. Maybe he's a peddler too. Maybe he sells kids."

Oliver pretended to be examining the maps some more.

Just before opening the door, she did a few jumping jacks and deep knee bends. Then she looked around at the nearly deserted parking lot, shrugged, and let out a long, cleansing scream. A few people glanced at her but not for long. Travelers accept odd sights and sounds, she guessed.

"There. Much better," she said to Oliver, who looked startled but strangely reassured by her scream. "Even big kids have to let off some steam."

"Maybe old men do too," he said, reaching into the clutter of the back seat to fish out his recorder. As soon as they found the exit for 294 and were safely on their way, he began to play. The next several miles glided by in the 6/8 time of a Bach gigue. Alison grinned into the bug-splattered windshield and felt the gently running rhythm weave her insides back together.

"Thank you," she said when he'd finished.

After Gary, and back into more relaxed countryside, Alison suggested Oliver take another nap. She tried not to reveal her alarm at how strange he appeared. "I can solo again now."

He nodded glumly but was peering surreptitiously into the back seat as he had earlier.

"Oliver." Alison took two deep breaths, but that didn't stop her heart from pounding. "Please. Go to sleep."

He mumbled something she didn't catch.

"What on earth are you looking at back there?" she asked at last.

"You can't see them, then? I was afraid of that . . . maybe *before* you could have. Before the tricksters turned on me. I'm truly sorry now that I left you out. You can forgive me for that, can't you, Alison?"

She stared ahead, so uneasy her vision began to blur, her fingertips to go numb. But she nodded her answer to his question. That was all he seemed to want just then — her forgiveness.

He turned forward to relax, but not to quiet down. He was mumbling again, a soft, rapid speech that reminded her of times before the Parkinson's had been under control. Hardly anyone could understand half of what he said.

"Sleep, sleep. Give it a rest," she said in a singsong voice that he'd often used on her when she was little. When he'd been sick, the Parkinson's gaining on him, he'd talked about sleep as something so precious. But not just any kind. "Not the kind," he'd say, "that takes you around the edges for hours, but the sinking-into-a-corner kind."

He often took naps, in those days, sitting in an easy chair by the window in his room. She'd look in on him often and once drew him there, using charcoal and her coarsest paper. He became a dark scribble against the bright rectangle.

Now in the car, he finally sank into his deep, safe sleep. But for one panicky moment, she again considered turning back. Maybe he was getting sicker. Maybe things wouldn't be better in Rockport. But Chicago seemed to her to have dropped a gigantic barrier between them and home. Three more days, she thought. That's all. Dad will know what to do. We can find a neurologist out there. That silver-haired foxy lady Mom found never seemed quite on top of things. Always leaving her office for days at a time. So sure of her precious drugs. Insistent that they were all he needed for now. Besides a mild sedative for insomnia, and a laxative. "His disease has not progressed very far yet," she had insisted, making Oliver feel, Alison was sure, like the breeding ground for some horror-movie organism.

They had been hurried out of her art deco office, Alison brimming with questions and knowing Oliver had some too. "She didn't say much about exercises, Mom," Alison had protested. "I've been reading about this thing, and exercise is one of the most important parts of his treatment. To get him moving better again."

But her mother had apparently been impressed, at least for the moment, by the neurologist's efficiency and her confidence, by the crowd of afflicted waiting outside her office, by the incessant ringing of her phone. "Here," she told Alison. "There's a brochure right here about exercises. Since you're such an expert all of a sudden, you be in charge of that part of his treatment."

Alison had grabbed the brochure and glared at her mother. Oliver had stood, looking from one to the other of them, occasionally lifting his hands and then dropping them to his sides again.

"Okay," her mother had concluded. "We're all set."

And, sure enough, within months Oliver had improved so much that he and Alison celebrated by wallpapering the bathroom — a celebration that dragged on for weeks, and of which they could find reminders in every rough-cut corner, every air bubble in the wallpaper.

Then suddenly came the secretive behavior and the closed door, his talking to himself, even sometimes whooping it up. And finally, the day last week she had heard him arguing, threatening, inside his room. Something was changing or maybe getting worse. She'd tried not to listen, but his door was on the way from her room to the kitchen.

Her mother had just come home from work. "Where is he?" she asked immediately. "Is he okay?"

"Napping," Alison said and stuck her face into the grocery bag her mother had placed on the counter.

"I don't think the doctor said he'd be needing so many naps all of a sudden," her mother said anxiously. "And then he can't sleep at night. I hear him wandering – "

"He said he took a long walk and it tuckered him out. We talked after I got home. 'All tuckered out,' he said, 'from my long walk.' " That truly sounded like something he'd say, Alison thought, but she left her face in the bag anyway. She could feel her mother looking at her.

"Something's definitely changed, honey. Don't you think? I mean beyond all the improvements in his walking and – "

"The tremors are better," Alison added, lifting her face.

"Yes, I know, but still . . ."

"He's fine, Mom. Don't keep looking for reasons to put him away. You keep saying how brilliant that doctor is. Oliver will be just fine." Alison hadn't meant to sound so angry and defensive. She knew she only made things worse when she talked to her mom that way.

"I don't want to 'put him away,' Alison. That's cruel of you to say. This residence I've been looking at, maybe I should – "

"It's always 'I should' this and that. Never '*we* should' anything. Never."

"He just shouldn't be alone so long each day. You agree with that, don't you?"

"What's for supper?" Alison said, angling the conversation away from Oliver.

"You know very well what's for supper. It says right here on the bulletin board. There's a hot dish that you were supposed to take out of the fridge and stick in the oven, half an hour ago." Her mother looked too tired to really get mad. Each item from the grocery bag might have weighed a ton the way she heaved it to the counter.

"Sorry, Mom. Let me do that. Go sit down."

"Once I sit, I'll never get up again. You know that. Let's get this meal over with."

Alison started pulling apart half a head of lettuce for salad. She couldn't help resenting her mother's tiredness. A lot of kids at school had mothers who worked outside the home and many of those were divorced too. It wasn't as though her mother had it tougher than everyone else.

Alison watched her as she went through her daily ritual of sniffing things in the refrigerator — open milk cartons, leftovers in plastic, vegetables for the salad. Her neck was long and curved gracefully, swanlike above small but firm round shoulders. Her back was so straight (except at times like this when she was tired) that it often made Alison want to run her hand up and down it, the way you do a perfectly sanded piece of wood. Her mother had the hips and legs of a long-distance runner even though she scarcely exercised at all. She was more lovely than Alison ever hoped to be. Her skin glowed without makeup, and the red hair, cut shoulder-length now, had a natural wave that Alison envied. They shared green eyes, but her mother's were a bright Irish green while Alison's were the color of a swamp.

Alison knew her mother could have all the dates she wanted. But she didn't seem to want many. "How's Richard?" she asked as they both chopped vegetables, and then added, "the lion-hearted."

"Fine, I guess," her mother answered with a barely perceptible smile. "What a little romantic you are."

"If that's what I am, where, exactly, is all the romance?"

"Inside your head," her mother answered. "Where it is for all us romantics."

"Who needs it?" Alison plopped a handful of radish slices into a salad bowl, wishing she could stop saying things she didn't mean, just because she knew her mother wanted to hear them. Placing a tomato wedge in her mouth, over her front teeth, she looked up and muttered, "Who'd want to kiss this anyway?"

Her mother responded with a polite laugh from pursed lips, a distracted *hm-m-m*. And Alison felt the sting of unexpected and unwarranted tears as she set the table. She knew it would be ridiculous to cry. And it might start another fight. "What're you bawling about now?" her mother might ask.

"You and me . . . and Dad," Alison would answer.

"Ah, the eternal triangle."

"And Oliver," she'd add. "If I lose him, I don't know what I'll do. Maybe kill myself."

But of course she had said none of those things. Instead she had talked to Molly the next day at school. And they had started planning the trip to Rockport.

"What're you two conspiring against?" Jordan had surprised them from behind. He rested his warm hand on Alison's shoulder — a natural, comfortable gesture that she appreciated. She was tempted only for a moment, to tell him everything.

"Let's see," he said. "I know how you feel about sports around here, Alison. Trying to ban soccer? Boycott the boys' gym?"

"I only resent soccer because you give that ball such undivided attention. And where does that leave me?" Alison did not often flirt with Jordan and the attempted diversion failed.

"Come on, what's up? You two looked so serious a minute ago."

Molly backed away. "Gotta run."

Alison thought for a moment, frantic. Then she hit on the perfect lie. "We're planning a surprise present for Mom. Her birthday's coming up."

"Really? Great. I'll help. Need some money?"

It had worked, of course. Jordan had jumped at the chance to do something for dear old Mom.

"Sure. A few bucks would help." And so she had let Jordan contribute, without his knowing it, to the trip to Rockport.

Chapter 6

SHE AND OLIVER sat in the car together for a full minute before moving or speaking. It was after 7:30 in the evening and food and beds awaited them; the orange sign flashed VACANCY invitingly above their heads. But still they did not move.

"Oliver. I can't seem to budge from this seat." Alison reached up slowly with her fingertips to prod her mouth because her words had come out wooden.

"You overdid it. That's for darn sure," he replied, sounding much better than she felt. He had, after all, napped a good part of the day; his skin remained sleep-puffy, but his voice sounded hearty, scooping out the fear he had planted in her earlier. He opened the door, letting in a refreshing slap of air, and carefully uncurled his body.

When her door opened she felt as though she might tumble out like a precariously stacked pile of blocks. "I just . . . wanted to stick to our plan," she said as she allowed her grandfather to extract her from the car. "That's all. We have to follow some kind of schedule. Don't we?" She looked back at the car, which seemed to contain a universe all its own.

"Should we unload? Or what?" Oliver looked helpless.

"Gee, I don't know." Alison's drooping arms mirrored his. When they simultaneously raised their shoulders into a shrug, palms lifted lazily, they both burst out laughing. "What a pair we are," she said. They laughed until that, too, wearied her.

"Let's eat first." She wiped her eyes and straightened up, extending her hand to Oliver. "We'll worry about our stuff and the room when we've regained our sanity. Food should help."

The restaurant was one of those with regal intentions; a few too many curlicued arches frowned at them and the chairs were the clumsy, heavy kind that took up too much space and probably bruised the waitresses' hipbones from time to time. The walls were dressed up in crimson paper that had surrendered most of its fuzziness to patrons' restless fingers. Three family-clusters sat mulling over their last bites of food and last sips of coffee.

No hostess appeared to back up the "Hostess Will Seat You" sign, so they seated themselves. This prompted a scowl from a passing waitress who balanced what looked like the entire kitchen on two scrawny middle-aged arms.

Alison and Oliver were still swallowing down laughter. She feared a worse kind of silliness could erupt at any moment, forcing them out of these civilized surroundings, to be consumed by the car forever.

"How do truck drivers do it?" she asked.

"How do truck drivers do what?" His eyes twinkled and she could see that she would have to be the serious one.

"How do they drive all day and night without going nuts?"

"They just get used to it, I guess. As we will. Probably about the time we get there." He laughed a hoarse laugh that ended up much too loud and a little unhealthy sounding. A nearby family turned five identically disapproving and suspicious faces in his direction. He mumbled an apology.

"Well, anyway," Alison said, "we made it almost to our goal. And boy, it'll feel good to stretch out on a bed, won't it?"

The harried waitress was ignoring them. "Do you suppose we're sitting here illegal-like," Oliver drawled, "and the local sheriff of this here town might jist lock us up for the night to teach us city-folk a lesson?"

Alison giggled, looking around for the hostess who still had not appeared. She walked over to the hostess stand to grab two menus and returned under the glare of the waitress — a woman who might have been born in a restaurant, delivered into this world in a starched pink uniform and a stiff, sprayed beehive of hair.

Oliver, in the meantime, helped himself to two glasses of ice water. Still standing, he shook a pill into his palm, deposited it between his lips and washed it down with his confiscated water. He could make anything look dignified, Alison thought.

They were both so hungry, they considered ordering three dinners between them but chose instead to order three desserts later.

Menus closed, they waited. Now the waitress had also disappeared. Since everyone else in the room appeared to have finished, only the two of them seemed in any distress. Alison began to covet the half-eaten plate of onion rings on a nearby table. Her stomach gave forth a hollow roar that made Oliver frown.

His eyes were dark with impatience. One fist began to thump against the table top, louder and louder. The silverware began to jump. "Somebody. PLEASE," he bellowed at last.

"Oliver," she said. "It's okay."

But he stood quickly, shaking off her hands that would have pulled him back into his seat. He threaded his way through tables and disappeared into the kitchen.

Almost immediately, he returned, cleared his throat, and calmly placed his napkin on his lap.

An incredibly hairy man with a beach-ball stomach not nearly hidden by his apron appeared to take their orders. He glanced furtively at Alison a few times and bounced lightly on the balls of his feet. "Sorry about the delay, folks," he said in a voice that was high-pitched and scratchy — a knife-scraping-a-plate kind of voice.

Alison almost laughed. How was it that such masculine bulk could not produce more of a sound?

"I've had two girls up and quit on me tonight." He glanced again at Alison with some apprehension. "Two in one night. Can you imagine?"

"Hard to believe," Alison said politely, in considerable discomfort. The man did not look at her as she was accustomed to being looked at. She checked her shirt for rips, the tip of her nose for something caught there.

After the cook wrote down their orders and slipped back into the kitchen, Alison asked, "Why did he look at me like that?"

"Because I told him my granddaughter was a hypoglycemic catastrophic and about to go into a dreadful fit if she didn't eat within five minutes."

"I'm a what?" Alison whispered loudly. "There's no such thing."

Oliver shrugged.

Crackers appeared miraculously within one minute, their

beverages within two, salads within three, and a thoughtful cup of soup, which neither of them had ordered, before the five minutes were up.

Their luggage and back-seat paraphernalia sat in one corner of the tidy motel room. It was so clean, in fact, it gave the impression of being fully laundered from top to bottom after each occupant. The smell was comforting in a careful, overbleached way.

"Well, here we are," Alison said, wandering around, examining the art reproductions on the walls. One was of Jesus sitting with some children, hand outstretched, sandaled feet relaxed beneath him. The other was a rather conventional still life with pottery and fruit, but the colors and depth warmed her.

"Did you say something?" Oliver asked.

"Nothing much."

He grunted. "You're going to call your mother now, aren't you?" His spirits seemed to have dwindled since his outburst in the restaurant. His dinner made him feel lethargic, he'd said, without finishing his apple pie.

Alison directed him toward the bed nearest the bathroom and bent to remove his shoes. "Maybe. And maybe tomorrow will be soon enough." She knew he was too tired to argue. "Suddenly I'm not all that tired," she said, and then wished she'd kept her mouth shut. Her energy seemed to press against her grandfather until he flattened into the beige bedspread. "I mean, I think I'll draw or read in bed, or something. Take your turn in the bathroom first if you like."

But he was already asleep, so quickly it frightened her. Had he passed out? But then he shifted into a tight zigzag, snorted, and smacked his lips.

"My hero," she said, smiling at his still form, and wrapping him into a bedspread cocoon.

Grabbing the nearest sketchpad and a pencil, she sat on his bed, near enough to feel warmth from his body, but far enough so she wouldn't disturb him with her drawing arm.

She sketched the children they had seen at the oasis, a crowd of joyous faces and strong bodies that began to multiply within itself, amoebalike. Two arms became four, four became eight. From the back of a snub-nosed profile popped its mirror image facing the opposite direction. The crowd became a multilimbed beast with dozens of smiling and shouting mouths, a hundred eyes like watchful warts.

Alison grinned and shivered as she shaded the beast. In the upper-right-hand corner she drew Oliver, sword and shield in hand, but he seemed to be trying to check something over his shoulder. It was hard to tell with what or whom Oliver was preparing to do battle.

"My hero," she repeated sadly, patting his spike of a shoulder.

She wondered, as she got ready for bed, whether she might actually need his heroics over the next few days. If their first day was any indication, this was going to be a long trip.

Chapter 7

THE NEXT MORNING Alison felt strong and refreshed, waking up at 6:00 to find Oliver already dressed and ready to go. The restaurant was just opening and they settled at the same table they'd had the night before. They shoveled in mouthfuls of delicious buttery eggs, toast, and hashbrowns, along with side orders of sausage.

There was no sign of last night's hairy cook, only a boy who looked like his son, already working on his pot belly and anxious expression. Oliver left him much too big a tip. "Best breakfast I ever ate," he explained to Alison, patting his stomach and sucking his teeth clean.

"Say," Oliver said when they were back on route, "what did your mom say last night?"

"What?"

"When you called her?"

"I didn't . . ." Alison cleared her throat. He'd been worse off last night than she'd thought. "I didn't get hold of her. She wasn't home."

"Really? That's hard to believe." Oliver stared at her for a long time.

"We can call her tonight. I doubt they'll accept a collect call at the bank, not for one of their tellers. And we can't spare the money."

"She's not a teller anymore."

"Well, whatever she is there."

Oliver frowned as they raced through the rest of Indiana. But then Ohio farmland seemed to go on forever, and the vast beauty of it seemed to distract him from Alison's deception. The land bumped and dipped in rich greens. The Triptik identified the farms as primarily for fruit production. Alison swelled with an earthy, if temporary, desire to be a fruit farmer someday. She could easily see herself propped against a roadside stand, selling her red, purple, and orange produce, plump points of color she'd put there as easily as if with her brush.

Crossing the Ohio line into Pennsylvania caused an excitement comparable to spotting land from a ship. *Pennsylvania* had an eastern sound to it, so unlike midwestern *Ohio*. She imagined that it even looked different, older, more colored by history.

Examining the map at lunch, they realized what a slim section of Pennsylvania they'd be crossing before hitting New York. Back in the car, they started to sing "New York, New York," Oliver doing his Sinatra imitation and Alison doing Liza Minelli. They didn't even mind that the air, for a while, sprinkled a fine, potent dust over their car and made it harder to breathe, much less sing.

The day rushed by in miles instead of minutes, interrupted only by the toll booths, which irritated Alison until Oliver made up a game, giving each attendant an appropriate name and family history. "That one's name is Neal Cripes, nicknamed Numbers. He used to be an accountant until his face started to break out in pimples shaped like numbers. He'd punch away on his calculator and the answer would pop up on his forehead." Alison laughed, already planning ahead for the next attendant.

Scenery became secondary to speed; a landmark was of interest only because it was farther along the page than the last one. Several times while she drove she became aware that her eyes had glazed over and her mind had wandered for what could have been several miles at a time. Groves of trees ahead of her flattened, forfeiting their third dimension. Outlines of hills fuzzed into sky and then drew themselves back again into proper clarity without her knowing why.

"Take over, will you, Oliver?" she said finally, pulling into a rest area.

While Oliver drove, Alison read about Buffalo, which they were about to bypass. Then she flipped ahead. Page after Triptik page. What a gigantic state New York turned out to be. They would be stopping for the night soon, with another two and a half pages of New York left for the next day. Albany would be almost the end of it, near their entry-way to Massachusetts. But then they would still be far from Rockport, which was on the opposite edge of the state. To distract herself from such depressing distances, she began to read aloud about towns and cities they would be passing.

"Fascinating," Oliver said at one point.

"Well, it is in a way. Maybe we should stop more. Look at all these tourist attractions they list here. We could get some history. You know?"

"What are you going to do, write a report about this trip for school?" He frowned. His jowls sagged so loose, the slightest bump made them quiver. She could remember actually touching his face only a few times in her life; he usually reacted as though her fingers deserved better.

64

They both were silent for the next several miles. When Oliver pulled into a rest stop, they got out of the car without looking at each other. Alison stretched and sighed, sniffing the pleasant, cool air but unable to shake the uneasiness coming from Oliver's direction.

"What's the matter with you, anyway?" she asked when they'd returned from their respective rest rooms.

"Are we here to sightsee or are we going to see your dad?"

"Both, it seems to me. Do you mind?"

"I don't know. I was just wondering. There's a lot to see in this part of the country. I know — I've been here before. We could eat, drink, and sleep history, if that's what you're after. Just so it's not because you're suddenly afraid to get where we're going."

"Afraid? To get to Rockport?"

"You heard me."

"You *are* crazy if you think that."

Alison had the sudden sense of being stared at. That's when she saw the girl standing near the exit from the rest area, her thumb extended boldly. Alison stared back at her; the girl was smiling, or smirking — Alison wasn't sure which, but she felt invaded. It was clear the girl had been watching and listening to their argument. "Do you mind?" Alison said to her.

The girl shrugged, checked her thumb as if to inspect its functioning and watched a car getting ready to take off in the direction she was headed. She was a black girl, plump and incredibly curved — prematurely, for she couldn't have been much older than Alison. Her face, except for the thick, rimless glasses, was that of a child — open, white-toothed, dimpled. Her short neat cap of hair and denim jumper gave her a no-nonsense look, contradicted only by her red high-topped sneakers.

Oliver was staring at her too now. He was frowning but Alison knew he was not disapproving of her, but rather of what she was doing. The dangers of hitchhiking was a favorite topic of his, and Alison sensed that one of Oliver's patented rescues was about to take place. There was something about this girl, however, that caused Alison to half expect her to resist the kind of rescue Oliver was about to offer as he approached her.

Alison started for the car in hopes that the girl would stay put, but just in the last minute several cars had passed her by without a glance. From behind the wheel, Alison watched the two of them talking. The girl hooked her hand onto one hip and stared openly into Oliver's face. Alison knew what he was saying – "dangerous practice . . . too many sickos on the road these days . . . young defenseless female," etc. The girl smiled then and spoke to him, looking about to grab him somewhere. Shake his hand? Throw her arms about his neck? Alison couldn't tell. Oliver backed away only slightly.

Another speech from Oliver – this time Alison couldn't guess what he was saying. Again the girl spoke. There was beginning to be an ease between them, almost an intimacy, that left Alison bewildered.

Finally, laughing about something the girl had said, Oliver picked up her army-green backpack and they approached the car. Taking their sweet time, Alison thought. She tried to look casual, even friendly. But all the while she wondered if the girl was as innocent as she looked. "You could've asked me about this first," she wanted to shout at Oliver as the girl settled into the back seat. Instead, she said, "I thought the back seat was too crowded as it is."

"Nonsense."

"I wasn't talking about luggage." Alison gave him a look that was meant to wipe away his smile.

But he conveniently forgot his back seat phobia. "Alison, this is Mira. Mira — Alison."

"How do you do," Alison said.

"I do real good, thanks," Mira said.

A smirk, Alison decided. To me she gives smirks. She rolled out of the rest area carefully. In control. "Where're you headed?"

"New York."

"City?"

"Of course, city. I'm already in the state, aren't I?"

"I just can't get over it," Oliver said, "how you made it all the way here from Detroit, hitching rides." Suddenly, this was an admirable feat instead of dangerous and stupid.

"Yes, sir." Mira exuded charm when speaking to Oliver. "Everyone was very nice to me," she added. "Oh, there was that strange woman who turned out to be an ex-cowboy in drag. But he was okay. He taught me how to yodel."

Before Mira could demonstrate, Alison asked, "What's waiting for you in New York?"

"You know — the usual. Fame, fortune, all that."

It was Alison's turn to smirk, but she said nothing.

"Are you an actress?" Oliver asked.

"Yes, sir. I am. I've been in half a dozen commercials, and three plays in our community theater."

"All that, and you're only what? Fifteen, like Alison?"

"Sixteen. That's funny, Mr. O'Brien. Most people guess I'm older. It's because of my —" She must have glanced downward or in some way indicated her chest.

Oliver squirmed in his seat.

"I'm not shy about it," Mira continued. "Wore a thirty-six C already when I was eleven. I can't afford to be self-conscious, now, can I?"

Alison glanced at her in the rearview mirror a few times. Her eyes were so dramatically enlarged by her glasses, they might have belonged to another face altogether. Hers was a face of surprises; it was beautiful even though it looked like it wasn't meant to be. Alison had to admit Mira probably could be an actress.

"Mira — that's a pretty name," Alison said. "Stage name?"

"No, Mama gave it to me. She thought I was sim-ply the image of her-self. Get it? Mira — mirror?"

"Cute," Alison said without thinking. "I mean, it's still a really pretty type . . . of . . . name." She could not entirely dismiss her initial suspicions of the girl.

"Thanks." Mira yawned and shifted around, apparently rearranging their belongings to better fit around her body.

"So, are you running away too?" Alison asked.

Oliver looked at Alison. "Is that what we're doing?"

Alison shrugged. "In a way."

Mira giggled. "I'm glad you told me you were related like you are, Mr. O'Brien. It would've freaked me out if you two were . . ."

She's forgetting, Alison thought with a grin, more and more who she's talking to. It's just a matter of time before Oliver gets fed up and drops her off. "We're not going to New York City, I'm afraid."

"That's okay. Wherever."

Oliver checked the maps. "Albany maybe?"

"Sure." Mira was all sweetness again. "That would be very kind of you."

"Okay," Oliver said. "We'll take you there, but only if

we can see you get on a bus. If you don't have the fare to New York, we'll lend it to you. Deal?"

"Whatever you say," Mira said. "Be sure to give me your address so I can send the money to you."

Alison sighed. How many pages of New York had she counted until Albany?

The gas-food-lodging sign directed them off the thruway. Another motel room (it looked like rain for sure this time), another coffee shop. A soggy salad and a hard potato added little to Alison's chicken dinner, but she was hungry enough to eat it all and then some. She noticed her jeans were beginning to bind her around the waist and chafe at her crotch.

"I'm gaining weight too," Oliver said as if reading her mind. "All that sitting. And eating."

Mira ordered only black coffee and munched on crackers, even after Oliver offered to buy her dinner.

"No, thank you. It's not money, really. I've got to lose some of this weight before I start making the rounds of auditions."

In spite of her tight jeans Alison delighted in the fact that at least *she* didn't have to starve herself like Mira was doing.

Oliver looked unconvinced and kept offering her bites of his meal. If it *was* money that was the problem, Alison had to hand it to Mira — she stuck to her crackers anyway.

"I'm built just like my mama," Mira said. "Now my grandma — she's the one who raised me — she was slim as a licorice whip. And pretty? Man. I always told her she's the one that should be headed for the theater." Mira shook her head and sipped her coffee.

Alison leaned forward to hear better. Mira had a husky, lyrical voice that often faded away as if she were only speaking to herself. If others wanted to listen, they'd have to work at it. For once Oliver listened without comment.

"Skinny as she was, she had the softest old lap. The best. You know, she always had something in her apron pocket for me: a flower, a shined-up penny, sometimes just a linty old lemon drop, but always something." Mira cleared her throat and stared into her coffee cup as if there were something foreign floating in it.

"She's gone now?" Oliver asked. His voice was as soft as the lap Mira had just described.

"Last month."

"I'm sorry, Mira." Oliver went back to his meal but only rearranged it with his fork.

"And your mother?" Alison asked.

Mira looked up and grinned. "Oh, she's alive and kicking all right. That's where I'm supposed to be now."

"She must be worried sick," Alison said and then caught Oliver's amused glance.

"Worried? Hell, no. Excuse me." Mira looked at Oliver. "It's just that she probably hasn't even noticed I'm gone yet. Or maybe she's downright relieved. I don't know."

Oliver's fork had slipped from his fingers.

"Listen, man." Mira shrugged. "Don't waste your sympathy on *me*. I do just fine on my own. I've got the name of an agent and I've got a place to crash till I get settled. See? So don't worry, you hear?" She reached across the table to pat Oliver's hand.

It was such a maternal pat, Alison had to smile. "Can I ask one more thing?"

Mira nodded at her, withdrawing her hand from Oliver and reaching for another free cracker.

"Where is your . . . father?"

Mira shrugged again.

Alison waited, and then asked, "You mean you don't know where he is?"

"Listen, man. I don't know *who* the s.o.b. is. Excuse me," she said again to Oliver, who by this time looked about to accordian up and slip to the floor, cartoon style.

Alison stood up. "I think we're all tired, right?" She grabbed Oliver's shoulders and discreetly helped him up.

"Tired, you bet," Mira said. "Listen — if it's okay, I'll stretch out in the back seat. Don't want to waste my bread on some fancy bed I don't need, you know. I could sleep standing on my head right now." She left without letting them protest.

Alison watched her broad back making its way to their car. "Oliver?"

"What else can we do?"

"But she might . . ."

"What? Steal it? Start the engine with a wire? You watch too much TV," he said. "It'll be fine. That girl is okay. Trust me."

"You, I trust." Alison didn't entirely appreciate the admiration in Oliver's voice when he spoke of Mira. Especially since she was having some trouble disliking the girl herself. "It's her I can't quite figure out yet."

They unloaded what they needed for the night from the car and registered for a room. Mira was already nearly asleep, curled into a ball in the back seat.

Chapter 8

A PHONE BOOTH, clouded top to bottom with greasy fingerprints, stood guard near their door. Oliver stopped and looked at it and then at Alison, who was trying not to stop.

"Alison," he said with quiet authority, "make your call."

"Oliver, I can't. I just can't call her. What do I say? 'Having a great time, wish you were here?' "

"Either you call your mother or I will. And who knows what I might let slip? Maybe our exact position – latitude and longitude."

She grinned at him gratefully. He was still playing the whole thing as a grand adventure. She knew most people in his situation would start to get exasperated by now, or worse, get bored, too grown-up for adventure.

"Oh, all right. Give me a quarter."

He gave her several and withdrew politely, as if the call were too personal for his ears.

"Hello, operator. I want to place a long-distance collect call to Tess O'Brien from Alison O'Brien."

Oliver's slouch was coming back, she noticed as she

watched him pace the parking lot. Probably from lack of exercise; she was sure letting him down in that department. Having given the phone number, she waited, impatient now to get the call over with. She had no clear idea what she was going to say.

"Hello. This is Tess O'Brien."

Both Alison and the operator began to jump in.

"— I am not home at the moment, but I will accept any call from or about my daughter, Alison. Please leave a message after the beep."

When on earth did she get a machine? Alison wondered.

The operator mumbled "Go ahead" a little uncertainly and then clicked off.

Even though she'd been waiting for it, the beep startled Alison. "Uh . . . hi, Mom. This is . . . me. We're doing just fine, Oliver and me. We're . . . we just wanted you to know that. Please don't worry. I know how you worry . . . is this still recording? Uh . . . good-bye for now. See you soon."

After hanging up, she regretted not adding "I love you." It used to come so easily for her. Every day, leaving for school: "Love you, Mom." Or at night, in bed, after their bedtime chats. It had always been a natural sign-off. And an understatement.

"Love *you*, Alison," her mother would say in return. "More than anything."

She glanced at their car and thought suddenly about Mira and *her* mother. She wondered how they said good night to each other, or if they even did.

The phone seemed to have more to offer her and she decided to call Jordan. His voice would sound very concerned and, probably, a little lonely. That would be nice to hear — someone else's loneliness.

She deposited the quarter and gave the operator Jordan's number, which luckily was easy to remember — almost all sevens. But Jordan wasn't home either, and, of course, his mother — sounding totally bewildered — declined the call. She must not know about my running away, Alison thought. Jordan didn't tell her.

She recalled that he was not at all close to his mother, being the eldest of three brothers, always depended on for everything and receiving little in return. Dependable, sensible, and nice. Yes, that was Jordan. But why should he be close to his own mother, when he had Allison's? They were probably together now somewhere. He could talk to her about soccer and her mother wouldn't yawn like Alison always did.

It was just as well he wasn't home for her call. He would have said, "Come home. We miss you." (We, as in Tess and I.) "Forget about your father. He's a jerk. He's not dependable and sensible and nice."

Alison leaned against the glass of the booth. No, that's not what he'd say at all. He'd probably say something like "Why didn't you tell me? We could have driven out to Rockport together. The three of us. It would've been fun."

She could picture him at the wheel of their car, his arm loosely draped over Alison's shoulder, and Oliver in the back seat, playing his recorder for them.

Jordan loved recorder music and had been after her for months to teach him how to play. "It's easy," she'd said, playing a quick C-major scale for him, showing him the logical progression of fingerings. But he hadn't paid attention. Instead he'd lifted two of her fingers away from the wood and kissed them lightly, a gesture that almost made her drop her recorder and her defenses. But she'd played the scale again, as if nothing unusual had happened.

74

Oliver started tapping sharply on the glass and she realized how foolish she must look, standing in that phone booth.

"Well?" he asked. "How was it?"

"It was a machine. She was out."

"A machine?"

"Probably another pajama party. We could be kidnaped or dead and she goes out."

"The operator let you talk?"

"Maybe this party is with poor Richard."

"Alison! Did you get to leave a message or not?"

"Yes, I did. But I have no idea what I said."

They inched toward the motel room.

"I thought," Oliver said, "that you might simply say 'We're out watching the snow melt.' "

Alison laughed, loosening much of the tension that had been knotting up in her chest. "I should have. I really should have."

"God, what a night that was," he said.

She sat down on the curb; he leaned against the phone booth. It was a warm evening but shot through with startling cool gusts from somewhere — possibly from within the grape-colored shadows of the hills.

"When I think about it now," she said, "I'm surprised she didn't ground me for a decade. I'd only had my permit a week or so. Picking you up from the library was the first errand I ran alone. And that, of course, was illegal but Mom was so sick. Throwing up and all."

"And there you were," he recalled. "Outside. When I'd been waiting inside. There you were — watching the snow melt."

It had been several days after a February blizzard. One that had left colossal drifts of snow, smoothed by the wind and unpunctured by human feet because of their depth.

75

Then those following days — thawing in the afternoon, freezing late at night — had left a glaze on the drifts as they shrank, shape intact. The street lamp by the library, an old-fashioned yellow lantern type, lit the glaze in a way that held Alison outside, staring. Because she could see one of the drifts melting, snowflake by snowflake. Each tiny particle, once lit by the lamp, snuffed itself out, calm as could be. Then another and another. The lamp-lit drift was twinkling, melting before her eyes.

When Oliver had found her she'd been angry at the intrusion — until she shared the sight with him. "I've got to get this down somehow. I have to make it permanent."

"I don't see how you could paint — "

"With a CAMERA," she shouted. "A movie camera. That's it, come on. They've got all kinds of things in the library."

Her excitement had been completely contagious. Oliver stood guard outside, as if the drift might be sabotaged in some way. Alison found a librarian to ask about movie cameras. He shook his head, but seemed intrigued by her idea, so she took him outside to have a look.

"The library doesn't have movie cameras, only projectors," the librarian explained as he stared at the drift. "But I have a camera."

So they had taken his house key, driven the half mile to his house, and found the camera and film where he'd instructed them to look.

But the project ended dismally. Even as they were filming, they all knew it wouldn't work. The light from the camera blanched out all the texture and killed the twinkling. And without the light, they knew the movie would be dark as night, any ordinary old night.

Thanking the librarian and returning reluctantly to the

car, Alison glanced at her watch. Almost three hours had passed since she'd left the house on a ten-minute errand.

"Mom'll kill us," she said, speeding all the way home. "She's probably already called the cops, telling them we've had an accident."

"Surely she called the library," Oliver said.

"But she could've gotten anybody there. Nobody knew where we were except Mr. Dolton. And he never said anything about a call."

"Don't worry. I'll take full responsibility."

"That's never done much good before, has it?" she asked.

And, of course, it hadn't that time either. Alison's mother had been trembling and red-faced. Too sick and panicky even to yell at them. They'd tried to explain, tried to tell her about the snow . . .

"Alison?" Oliver said now. "It's time to go into the room, Chief."

"I guess," she said, standing up to stretch and dig out the room key. "We gave Mom kind of a practice run that night. For what we're doing now."

"Maybe so," Oliver said. "She must be pretty calm if she bought that machine and went out for the evening."

"Probably 'the movement' needed her."

"Imagine — buying that thing just for us."

"Yeh, that stupid machine will probably be my birthday present this year," Alison said and then shrugged. "Oh well. I'm glad she's not all in a panic."

"Not yet anyway," he added as they entered the unlit room.

Chapter 9

"*I* THINK I'LL run a mile or two," Alison said after they'd turned on a lamp. The room felt like a tomb to her.

"Thought you were tired."

"It's the wrong kind of tired," she said.

Oliver was looking around, clenching and unclenching his hands. "Maybe you'd better not," he said. "I mean, you only ate a short time ago. And besides, it'll get dark soon."

"I'll be back before it gets dark. I've got to get some exercise." Digging out her running shoes and sweatclothes, she was vaguely aware that Oliver was not moving, except for his hands. "You okay?" she asked.

He nodded. "Just tired."

"I'll stay if you want."

He shook his head and moved on to the bathroom. He seemed to be fighting his slouch and the effect was one of stubborn stiffness.

She changed quickly and listened at the bathroom door. Maybe I shouldn't leave, she thought. But he's been feeling so good all day. Everybody has a right to get tired.

The long drive was not good for him, that was becoming more obvious. "Oliver? How about if I just walk and you come with me? You should be exercising too. Remember what . . . Oliver?"

"Go ahead and run, Chief. You'll get back faster. I'm going to bed."

As soon as she closed the motel room door behind her, she breathed better. It was beginning to drizzle slightly, but she didn't mind. It felt so good to be moving, even if she had eaten too much too recently, that she refused to acknowledge the stomachache she was giving herself. But when her breathing became painful as well, she stopped, shaking out stiff knees and ankles. She sat down on the soft shoulder of the highway which would take her into town if she wanted to see it.

The hills were engulfed in their shadows now, back-lit by the sinking sun. The breeze kicked up an insect-sized dust storm on one side of the road, while on the other, a rowdy crowd of wildflowers was clamoring for every drop of rain as well as for her attention. So much to see and touch. There were plenty of wildflowers in Minnesota. But that did not keep her from wanting to see these and much more.

What harm could a little sightseeing do? If Oliver thought she really was afraid to get to Rockport, maybe he *was* slipping. The letters and cards she'd been getting made her dad sound nice enough. Concerned about her, even if it had taken him too long to get around to it. He was proud of her talent, his major contribution to her gene pool.

A chill raced up her backbone. She was soaked with rain and sweat. Her stomach was still in shock from being filled to its limit and then shaken up so mercilessly.

"My work is going well here," her dad had written

recently. "I've been meeting people I can talk to, really talk to, for the first time in years. One of them has a daughter about your age. She's pretty, like you, and she's talented, but not as talented as you are. I've shown her some of the pictures you've sent me. She asked why you like birds so much and I told her I didn't know. The landscape you did of Lake of the Isles is my favorite yet. I love the way you blended the tiny figures of joggers and roller-skaters into the fabric of the scene. So natural, they could be colorful shrubs, or maybe some city wildlife. You could use some work in sky coloration though . . ."

Typical. She rubbed her face, mixing rainwater with the oil of her skin to make a lotion slickness. It was so typical for her father and mother to see something so differently. Her mother had loved that sky; it was the best thing about the Lake of the Isles watercolor for her.

"It shows your imagination, Alison," she had said. "Your limitless imagination is what makes you especially gifted, better than . . . well, than most. It looks like you've spilled a little of it into this sky. Opened your mind and spilled a bit of its contents. Just enough."

Alison had re-examined the sky of her picture, a little flustered by her mother's reaction to it. She had started it with a cool, respectable mixture of blues and wispy white. But then other colors came into play—reds and browns and, of all things, some scratches of green, as if cut into the scene by some windblown leaves.

She had painted that particular watercolor one day during spring vacation, when the budding and greening of everything had filled her head to bursting. She had to try to get something on paper, something to ease the tension that beauty so often created in her. Lake of the Isles had always been a favorite spot for both her and her mother. It's been sort of their spot, for the first several springs residing in Alison's memory.

Upon examining the watercolor early the following morning, her mother had offered the flattering remarks about her daughter's imagination, and then had surprised Alison, and probably herself, by calling the bank to say she was sick. "Let's go there, to the park, and take a day like we used to have." She'd said "take" in the "steal" sense of the word, making Alison a little uneasy but nonetheless grateful.

Walking along the paved path in the park, her mother had cupped her hand around Alison's shoulder, now at the same height as her own. They observed the scene together, the breathless, spring-sick people at play around them.

It was at moments like this, too few recently, that Alison loved her mother more than she could say. Moments when there was no need to say anything, no way to trespass across each other's needs because their needs were in perfect union. They simply wanted to be together, skin lightly brushing skin. Friends, but more than that. Much more. That was why their fights could be so terrible.

She tried to recapture their latest fight, the one precipitated by Raoul and ending with Alison's assurance that she, at least, was smart enough to use contraceptives. But her earlier view of it eluded her. She began to understand now why her mother's control had crumbled, why she'd given Alison such a look of helplessness when she raised her hand to slap her.

Her mother had gotten married because, as Alison had so indelicately put it, she'd been a dopey kid herself. And look at the results: a dead baby, a runaway husband, and now a runaway daughter. And that odd mysterious thing she had said about having no generation — young girls with babies, who worked full-time and did not go to college, were not often included in peace marches or anything else that might have identified them as a part of the glorified sixties. Even Alison knew that. She should always have known. Maybe that was why the women's movement had become so crucial to her mother in the last few years.

Alison closed her eyes. It was raining harder now, mixing with her tears. She missed her mother fiercely, not as she'd seen her last: weary and desperate to recapture something before her youth had escaped her. She didn't much like feeling sorry for her own mother. No, she missed the mother she had had for twelve or so years, with whom she could share her own dreams. The mother she never would have considered running away from, worrying, or deceiving as she had done.

Alison stood up, pulled the wet sweatpants from her thighs and jogged slowly back toward the motel.

She knew something was wrong before she'd even crossed the parking lot. The door to their motel room was wide open, a bright rectangle in the long line of snugly closed doors. Running now, she grew terrified that the room would be empty, or worse. Maybe Mira really was dangerous. Or maybe . . .

"Listen, bud," a strange voice was shouting, "you want me to call the cops or not?"

She reached the door, panting. Sweat stung her eyes and she tried to blink them clear. Mira was nowhere in sight. But there was Oliver, sitting on his bed in his striped pajamas, one slipper clutched in his right hand. The manager of the motel was standing over him, hands on his hips. He was sweating too, darkening the back of his shirt and a V on the seat of his pants.

"Alison," Oliver said, lowering his slipper-weapon. "Thank God you're back."

"Where was ya?" The manager turned on her. "This crazy old coot was trying to get the cops out here. Says there was intruders. I come in here and this is what I see —" He swept a long muscular arm from one corner of the room to the other. "Nothin'. Nobody. All I need is to get all the other people here riled and have some damn report writ up against me."

He glared at Alison. "Troublemakers like you I can do without. Any more trouble and you can get out, the both of you."

Alison felt herself flush with anger. "I'm sorry, sir, if there was a little trouble, but —"

"He was pounding on doors, girlie. It's gettin' dark outside and this loony starts pounding on doors. Lucky for him, the office is only two doors down. I stop him banging and he says to me to call the cops. And that's just what I'll do if there's another peep outta you." He started to slam the door behind him as he left and then caught it just in time to prevent the noise.

"Nice man," Oliver said quietly.

"What on earth happened here?"

He shook his head. "I'm not exactly sure."

Her breathing had slowed finally and she tried to stay as calm as possible. What if the police had come? They would have asked to see identification, such as nonexistent drivers' licenses. They would have tried to get Oliver to a doctor. They surely would have called her mother. She pushed back the thought of policemen snooping around, way back with all the panic she'd felt running across the parking lot. "Just tell me as best you can. Was it a bad dream or something?"

He pointed toward her bed, which was slightly mussed.

"They were there. It was no dream. They aren't going to let us sleep here tonight."

Knowing better than to sit on her own bed just then, she sat on his. "Who was there?"

"They're small, but that doesn't mean a thing. There're too many of them. And they seem to know everything."

"Oliver — "

"They know what foods I should eat and what foods give me gas. They were laughing at me. Or maybe it was because they know Gerard will be shocked at how I look. He'll think I'm sick and dying. They think that's funny too."

Alison started to tremble. Somebody help me, she wanted to shout. But she took a few deep breaths. After all, she'd suspected for weeks that he'd "found" some strange people, but she'd half convinced herself they'd been real. Or real enough. "Tell me about them. Please."

"Little people. Funny little people. As plain as I see you now."

"Little people?"

"Used to give me pleasure, kept me company in a way. Such a funny bunch, back in my room." He looked up at Alison, nervous but apparently relieved to be talking about them. "They seemed to be partying . . . I don't know. I even started to name a few of them. They were my friends."

Alison recalled the jealousy she'd felt a few times outside his room, listening to him with his "friends."

"Now . . . it's different." His voice thinned to a thread. "They disappear for hours at a time and then . . . back again, watching me. I'm never sure what they're up to. I just wish they'd let you see them too, Alison. I just wish . . ." His eyes were moist and bloodshot. They searched her for what she couldn't give him. Not this time.

She looked at her bed again and then down at her hands. She wanted to peek under the bed but she didn't. It was so unfair. He had seen her snowdrift melting, so easily. Why couldn't she see these little people? Even for a moment?

"Oliver, we're both tired, now. We'll talk about it tomorrow. Go to sleep."

She tucked him into bed, slipped into the bathroom, sat on the edge of the tub and started to cry. She cried all the while she pulled off soggy clothing. Shivering in a motel bathroom somewhere in New York State, she felt a loneliness she had never known possible.

Chapter 10

ALISON WANTED to scream at Oliver to pull himself together, but she realized how selfish that would be. He couldn't help it; he wasn't deliberately letting her down any more than she was deliberately letting him down. Maybe it was something in their genes – her father's and grandfather's. A weakness. But that was unfair too.

He needed her to help him, but it was an effort for her just to move, just to turn on the water, lift one knee and then the other to step into the tub, to stand under the shower.

She let the water take over all control. She closed her eyes, breathed through her mouth and spit out warm water. Her hair tickled between her shoulder blades. I'll stay in here long enough for him to go peacefully to sleep, she told herself. She felt guilty, so guilty for leaving him out there, for not having found the means to console him. She wondered if water could rinse away guilt if she stood under it' long enough.

But she emerged from the bathroom several minutes later, only cleaned of sweat and mud. Oliver was asleep.

She removed the slipper still clutched in his hand and covered him up to his chin. She kissed his cheek, and then wiped away the water that had dripped from her hair. He frowned but did not wake up.

She climbed back into her jeans and shirt and a few minutes later found herself standing by their car. Mira's face was indistinguishable within the massive lump in the back seat. Alison opened the door quietly but jumped when Mira abruptly woke up in the light.

"Shoot," Mira said. "You nearly scared me half to death."

"Sorry." Alison climbed into the front seat and closed the door, welcoming the darkness.

After a few moments, Mira asked, "What's up?"

Alison sniffed.

"You been crying about something?"

"Sort of," Alison said.

"Something heavy, huh?"

Alison detected not an ounce of the nastiness she thought she'd seen in Mira before. Nighttime changed things. She'd often noticed that.

"Is it the old man?"

Alison still had trouble dislodging words from her tight throat. She was lonely. Couldn't that be enough reason to be out there with this stranger?

"Does he . . . uh . . . get rough with you? I mean . . . you know, abusive?"

Alison laughed out loud, loosening up the words at last. "Oliver? Are you kidding?" But she sensed Mira pulling away again. "I'm sorry for laughing, but if you knew him better, you'd know how funny that is."

"Well, if you can't talk about it . . ."

Alison waited for some sign of Mira's going back to sleep, but she still felt her attention. "Didn't you hear all the commotion earlier? The manager coming by our room and all?"

"No. Nothing."

"Well, Oliver was acting sort of . . . I don't know. Do you think he could be . . . crazy?"

"Crazy? Not a bit. And I've *seen* crazy, believe me."

"What if I told you he sees things — people? Little people. And they sort of frighten him."

"Um-m-m. How little? Like midgets or just sort of below average?"

"I'm not sure. Why? Does it matter?"

Mira sighed, apparently choosing to ignore that question. "Otherwise he's okay, though? Like he was at dinner?"

"Better even. He was tired at dinner. And the pills hadn't had time to take effect yet."

"Oh, yeah? Pills? What kind of pills?"

"He has Parkinson's disease."

"Oh, I get it. Isn't that the thing when you shake all over and drool and get old real fast?"

"Sort of," Alison replied uneasily.

"Well, then it's simple. You take him to a doctor."

"He has a doctor, back home. What I can't seem to figure out is what to do right now."

Mira shifted her body around with a grunt and a sigh. Alison waited. At last Mira spoke.

"Well, all I can tell you is that when my mama would act crazy, I sometimes could just sort of talk her out of it, show her there was nothing there that could hurt her, yell at her to shake her up, you know?"

Alison nodded vigorously enough to be seen in the dark.

"You headed anywhere in particular?" Mira asked.

"Rockport, Massachusetts. To my dad's."

"He know you're coming?"

Alison hesitated. "No. Not exactly."

Mira was silent.

"He'll be glad, though. You should read his letters to me . . . and he'll know what to do about Oliver. He's *his* father, you know. It'll be great."

"Sounds great." Mira yawned and scratched herself somewhere. "Listen . . ."

"Yeah, I'll let you get back to sleep." Alison opened the door and they blinked at each other in the harsh light. "Thanks."

"My pleasure."

"Mira?"

"What?"

Alison closed the door again, readmitting them to darkness. "What did you mean before, about your mother acting crazy?"

"Oh, that. She's . . . well, frankly, she's a drunk."

"She's a—?"

"Now I don't blame her. Not a bit. I know it's an illness like diabetes and all. I've heard enough social workers go on about that shi— about alcoholism. I feel plenty sorry for Mama. Even that time . . . that time when I was little and she forgot and sat me down on that hot stove. It hurt like hell, but it was Mama who was hurting the worst. The point is, she's no mother when she drinks and since she's drinking now, forget it."

Alison felt the tears threatening to return. "I . . . don't know what to say, Mira."

" 'Say good night, Gracie.' "

"What?"

"Never mind. Listen, man. I bared my soul. You tell me now — what's the story with your mama? Why'd you split?"

"Oh, nothing much, I suppose. She's not a drunk or

anything and she doesn't hit me, if that's what you mean."

"Does she chase around with men?"

Alison laughed. "No."

"Does she lie to you?"

"No. Not exactly. She's hidden things from me though."

"Can you talk to her, usually?"

"Used to."

"Does she love you?"

Alison sat silent, not doubting the answer for a moment but having trouble getting it out. Finally she nodded.

"Yes?" Mira asked. "Well—" she laughed her slowest, huskiest laugh. "It's a wonder you stuck with that mean lowdown bitch as long as you did."

Alison smiled in spite of herself. She said good night and left Mira to her uncomfortable bed and to her certainty about the world. In a way she regretted not having a horror story about her mother to give to Mira. It would have given them something in common. But now an unwelcome feeling of pride was wriggling its way into the picture. Her mother was, in many ways, someone to be proud of, someone Mira would probably be grateful to have for a mother.

Okay, she told herself. So I ran away from a mother who's not a monster. So what? Does that make her any less impossible for me to deal with right now? And maybe I do miss her. A lot. And maybe I do want to try to live with her again. Sometime. But that doesn't get me any closer to my dad. This trip is far from over and if it helps me to get there, then I'll just have to stay angry with her. Angry as hell, whether she's a monster or a saint.

Oliver was wide-awake again when she returned to him. He looked worried but was riveted to his bed. "Forgot my sleeping pill," he said. "I want to be asleep if they come back. They leave me alone when I'm asleep. Usually."

Alison flicked on the overhead light, which gave the room an odd, orange glow. "There is nobody here," she said loudly, throwing all her bedclothes onto the floor, crouching to look under the bed and then moving the few pieces of furniture around. "See? Nobody."

"You think I'm nuts, don't you?" he asked.

"No. Definitely not. Just tired. And confused."

"I don't know." He shook his head.

"I don't know either," she said, "about any little people. But I do know you're not nuts, any more than you're weak or I'm helpless. Or . . . look, Oliver." She sat down next to him. "I believe you see these things, these people, and we're going to get to the bottom of it. As soon as we get to Dad's . . ."

He was watching her mouth as she spoke, his eyelids lowered like those of a shamefaced child. His lips were white, his face streaked with red. "But . . . but they . . . don't like me anymore. And they certainly don't like you."

Alison scowled at him. "Who? Oh . . . well, I don't care. They can't hurt us."

"Look at me," he said wearily. "Look at what they can do."

"But most of the time, Oliver, you're still good as new. The pills are working. And I really think this trip could be good for you. You can . . . we can handle this. I know it."

She watched as he absorbed that for a while. She could see him drawing strength from her, an intravenous gift from her to him. She watched and waited.

Then she leaned over to plant a wet kiss on his forehead.

Sliding quickly off the bed, he said, "Get that damn cold wet hair away from me already."

"Okay, okay. I'll tell you what. We're not really sleepy right now. So let's play some duets. Better than sedatives any day." Without letting him reply she handed him his recorder and sat down next to him with hers. They shared the Telemann book. She could feel his arm next to hers, the muscles working as his fingers moved, straining for the fast movements, massaging the notes in the slow movement.

The moist, breath-warmed wood of their recorders gave off a comforting smell that she could still detect later as she fell asleep.

Chapter 11

THE NEXT MORNING, Alison could not seem to wake up. She was aware of Oliver's voice, of the sound of drapes being opened to usher in the sun. But still she clung to the dark mustiness of sleep that felt as deep as the earth's core. No more driving, no more absent fathers or angry mothers, no more little people mussing her bed. None of that. Go away, she wanted to tell Oliver, but opening her mouth might be the very thing that would make her let go of sleep.

It was a sharp swat on her behind that finally did it. "WAKE UP." It was Mira, who had a mouth on her in the morning that could rouse a whole town. Alison had to stop and think who this girl was.

Their breakfast was hurried and hard to digest. Mira forfeited seventy-five cents for soggy toast, and this, plus coffee, seemed to satisfy her so completely that Alison felt like a glutton with her own breakfast. They knew better than to offer her some of their food.

They re-entered the New York State Thruway at 7:45, Alison at the wheel, silent but fully awake now. It won't be much longer now, she reminded herself.

It was another glorious summer morning, the third in a row, surely a good omen. She was wearing cut-off jeans now, and another from her stack of T-shirts. The radio forecast a high of 80 degrees. Perfect. This was where she was supposed to be, she told herself. Glancing at Oliver, she tried to reassure him too, but he looked rested and eager for the day without her help.

"Let's play a game," he suggested. "The time will pass quicker."

"What about that game we played when I was little," Alison asked. "I went on a trip and in my bag I packed a . . . an agitated alligator."

"I went on a trip," Oliver responded, "and in my bag I packed an agitated alligator and a billiard ball."

"I went on a trip," Mira began with a giggle, "and in my bag I packed an agitated alligator, a billiard ball, and a . . . carton of castaways."

When it was Mira's turn for "I," she mumbled to herself for a while. Then, glancing down at her chest, she said, "I know! I'll pretend I'm Alison here and take my itty-bitty . . . oh, never mind."

Oliver and Alison roared with laughter, but eventually they settled on itty-bitty igloos instead. Alison was strangely pleased; there had been a time when she was very self-conscious of her small breasts. Mira seemed to have an ability to minimize problems, for herself and anyone around her.

Oliver was first to get stumped in the game. He couldn't for the life of him remember Mira's lumpy-shirted limp wrists. They played to Z anyway, cheating repeatedly along the way.

The morning slipped by and they chose to stop for gas and lunch between Chittenango and Canastota. "We'd like cheeseburgers, Cokes, and coconut cream pie," Oliver ordered as solemnly as he could. "And a carton of cast-aways," Mira added. They all giggled after the bewildered waitress left them.

During lunch, Mira treated them to her imitation of some of the uptight white teachers she'd had along the way and told them how she, acting polite as could be, had still been the one behind every revolution in the classroom.

Mira made it possible to laugh even at the fact that she'd gone to what she called "re-tard school" for a year because of her terrible eyesight and because she had mild dyslexia. "But I showed them," she said. "Taught my*self* to read. It knocked their silk stockings right off. Ended up in gifted programs and been doing for my*self* ever since."

Oliver had rarely been so taken by anyone that Alison could remember. He listened as if transfixed by Mira's shining teeth. She knew that yesterday she would've been jealous.

They stopped off, reluctantly, at the bus depot in Albany.

"Now, Mira, you're sure you're going to be okay?" Oliver looked as though he might lock all the car doors and insist that she stay with them the rest of the way to Rock-port.

Mira did not answer. Instead she gave Alison a flashy grin.

"She'll be fine," Alison said for her. "Great, even. If anyone can take care of herself, it's Mira."

"You're not doing too bad either, man."

Alison felt herself blush. "Except, maybe I jump to conclusions sometimes about people."

"Sometimes," Mira said, grasping her belongings and opening her door, "it's not such a bad idea. Take care now." She gave Oliver a quick peck on the cheek and was gone almost as suddenly as she'd appeared the day before.

Alison frowned and pulled the car out of the depot parking lot. "We should've gotten her address or given her ours or something."

Oliver nodded and glanced at the back seat.

"Little people back there again?"

"No. I was just noticing the empty space she left. Addresses — yes, that would've been the thing to do. Why on earth didn't we think of it?"

"Maybe," Alison said with a smile big enough, she hoped, to wipe out some of the regrets, "we'll see her starring in a play someday."

"Of that," Oliver said, "I have little doubt." After a pause and another glance behind him, he added, "Or at least *you* will."

It was on a late-afternoon pit stop that they saw the woman who looked like Theta Rae. They were drinking Cokes and cooling off in an air-conditioned café. "Oliver," Alison whispered and pointed discreetly to the elderly woman who had just come in. "Is that who I think it is?"

Oliver stared at the woman while he took his pills, swallowed, winced. She sat down in a booth not far from theirs. She was alone and appeared to be rummaging through her purse for something. "Couldn't be," he announced finally, but he did not look certain.

"It's been a few years," Alison reminded him. "She doesn't look any older."

"Theta Rae wouldn't look any older," he said, shaking his head and reaching for a cracker. The woman had noticed his staring but she showed no recognition. Only a kind of amusement. Or was she flirting?

"That definitely isn't Theta Rae, Oliver. Although she could be related. Don't you think?"

They had met Theta Rae about four years ago. Alison was eleven when her mother had announced that it was time she took piano lessons.

"Mother," Alison had protested, "I'm too old for that."

Her mother looked astonished.

"Most of the kids have been taking piano since they were four or five."

"Don't be ridiculous," her mother said.

"It's true. I swear it. They start real early and are playing Beethoven and Chopin by the time they're my age. Please, Mom. I don't want piano lessons. Everyone would laugh at me."

"Alison, I don't know what kids you're talking about, but I do know that you must have a basic knowledge of the keyboard to . . . to . . ."

"To what?" Alison asked.

"Well, I don't know. I've always wished I could play. It's important, that's all."

"Well, you should have thought of it earlier then."

Her mother wrapped her slender powder-scented arms around Alison. "Honey, you're still plenty young. And I know you'll catch on quick. You'll love it. Just wait and see."

They bought an old piano for eighty-five dollars. "A real bargain," her mother announced proudly. The "bargain" was a moody old upright whose middle C and a few other keys liked to stick, except when the piano repairman came.

Theta Rae Frost arrived for that first Saturday afternoon lesson and Alison nearly groaned out loud. She had expected some young musician-type in jeans with messy hair, humming to herself and pounding feverishly on the piano keys. "Let us begin with some easy Chopin," the musician would say and let her magnificent, short-nailed fingers prowl across the keys effortlessly, beautifully.

Instead, there was Theta Rae. One of those women inching into her sixties so gracefully it was almost spooky. She had a figure like Alison's mother's. Narrow waist, straight back, tight-skinned neck. Her feet were tiny and neat in their size 4 wedgies, so high that her heels sat almost directly above the balls of her feet. This gave her a curious, bent-kneed, clenched-rear kind of walk that Alison tried out once and nearly crippled herself. Theta Rae's smoothly styled, white-divinity hair appeared impervious to wind or rain, and she always wore eyeglasses that matched her outfit and shoes.

"This is middle C," Theta Rae began, laying a perfectly manicured forefinger on the key which, naturally, refused to sound. She tried again, unruffled. Still no sound. Alison thought she heard a sickly ping from somewhere inside the workings.

"Well," a tight smile from Theta Rae, "anyway, middle C is your best friend. Your home sweet home. It should point right to your middle." One oval fingernail poked gently into Alison's stomach, which she realized she'd been holding in unnaturally since her teacher had arrived.

To Alison's dismay, her first lesson ended without her venturing beyond the first five notes of the C-major scale. "At this rate," she told her mother, "I'll be Theta Rae's age before I can play Chopin."

Her mother merely smiled, seeming to tuck a secret inside her cheeks.

Every Saturday for nearly two months was much the same. Theta Rae always wore one of three suits — tailored jackets, straight skirts, made out of some woven fabric that Alison could not name. Sitting next to her on the bench, Alison wanted to rub her fingers across the nubby surface of this fabric each time before touching the cold, untextured keys.

It struck her almost immediately that she and Theta Rae had been thrown into a very strange relationship. Intimate, in a way. Sitting side by side on the piano bench most of the time, shoulders lightly touching, Alison could detect the scent of whatever Theta Rae had just eaten. She could sniff out evidences of lifestyle, such as stale smoke, wet dogs, and fried onions, even through the layer upon layer of hairspray. She memorized every hair and freckle on Theta Rae's hands, the unique jut of her wrist bone. But still, she always felt in the presence of a stranger. It was disquieting, and it distracted her from the task at hand, namely learning to play piano.

By the time Alison was torturing "Lightly Row" from the reluctant keys, everything had turned suddenly worse. Oliver and Theta Rae had met and, it seemed, fallen in love. Not that they did anything about it except blush and stutter and hold Alison captive between them.

Theta Rae Frost had never married, but Oliver would not allow any reference to her as an old maid. He started sitting in on most of the lessons, always coughing at the time of Alison's most intense concentration. Her fingers would then stiffen, aware of his attentive presence.

"Look, Oliver," she had said one day after weeks of such foolishness. "Ask her for a date and get it over with."

"Date? Don't be such a child," Oliver answered, paging through a women's magazine as if interested in it.

"Well, do something, for heaven's sake. Call her up and ask her over for dinner, then."

Oliver tossed the magazine aside and floated from the room, oblivious to Alison's dilemma.

"If I never play Chopin, it will be all your fault," she shouted after him.

Months went by much the same. Oliver and Theta Rae

were finally exchanging scraps of small talk. Always, of course, with Alison fidgeting at the piano, waiting.

Then one day Theta Rae mentioned a recital she wanted to go to the next evening. Oliver cleared his throat but said nothing.

"That sounds like a good recital, Oliver," Alison said. "Just the kind of music you like most."

"Geez, it's been hot lately, hasn't it?" Oliver asked.

Alison stared at him. Had she missed something, or was he being impossible?

"What I need right now is a beer," he continued. "How about you, Miss Frost?"

Theta Rae declined politely, straightened her unrumpled skirt, touched her hair and left.

"Oliver, you blew it. I can't believe you offered her a beer instead of asking her out."

"It *is* a very hot day," he said as if that explained everything perfectly. "There's nothing like a beer – "

"She wanted you to take her to that recital."

His eyes widened in hopeless innocence. "Don't be silly. What would she see in an old man like me?"

Alison gave up. She still couldn't play the piano and she'd grown to dread Saturdays almost as much as going to the dentist.

Quitting was by mutual consent. They'd given it a year. Alison was discouraged and unresponsive. Theta Rae declared her a child with scarcely an ounce of musical aptitude. (To her, recorder music didn't count.) Alison's mother sighed a lot for several days, and then sold the piano, which left marks in the carpeting that never quite disappeared.

Alison had felt as marked by the experience as the carpeting. And Oliver had succumbed to a depression that had lasted for weeks (this was shortly before the Parkinson's symptoms began to appear).

"Were you in love with Theta Rae Frost?" she asked Oliver while they dawdled over the last few fizzy drops of Coke.

"Love?"

She hoped he wouldn't launch into some sweeping, evasive definition of love.

"No," he answered after his straw gave him nothing but noisy air. "It was not love. I'd say it was more like lust."

Alison bit down hard on her straw. After all these years, he could still astonish her.

"I simply wanted to watch her kick off those ridiculous shoes and muss up that hair."

Alison was stifling giggles because he was being so serious.

"Are you shocked?" he asked.

Alison shook her head. "More like guilt-ridden."

"For what?"

"For being so unmusical. Maybe if she'd come around longer, you two would have gotten together, or something."

Oliver gave an exasperated sigh. "And what makes you so sure we didn't?"

"What?"

"That's the one thing I've hated about living with you and your mother. You're both so damn determined that I turn into an overgrown baby, depending on you, asking your permission, telling you everything."

"But . . . but we didn't —"

"You've made it tough, but I've managed to keep a few tricks up my sleeve. I went out with that woman. Twice."

Alison felt surprised and delighted and upset all at the same time. She realized he was right — they had been treating him like a kid sometimes. "How . . . did it go? With Theta Rae?" She gave him an encouraging, but she was sure *not* a patronizing, smile.

"Terrible," he grumbled. "But that's not the point."

"The point is, you did it. And we didn't even have to know. Right?"

"Right. I have . . . desires, you know. Just like any other grown man. Age and illness don't have to . . . well, deaden everything."

"I know that."

"It's strange, but, in a way, I was kind of looking forward to that senior citizen residence. At least there would have been people there my own age."

Alison couldn't believe what she was hearing. "You mean —"

"Now don't go getting hurt. I don't mean I've been aching to leave you two. Nothing like that. It's just that I was beginning to see some advantages. For everybody. Can you understand that?"

Alison swallowed and nodded. "I guess it was . . . pretty dumb of me to drag you off like this, then. I guess . . . I was doing it for me, not for you, after all."

"Not to worry, Chief. It's all turning out fine. You've put a spark back into me that was about out. We're going to see your dad, right?"

Alison relaxed again. "Right."

The woman who looked like Theta Rae was returning from the ladies' room. Alison hesitated, but then asked what she had to ask. "Were there others? Other . . . dates we didn't know about?" In a way she hoped there had been. She waited for him to say, "Hell, yes. Dozens." And she could say in a very grown-up way, "Good for you!"

He only looked at her. "Not really. Well, there was this

cute clerk at the grocery store. We used to flirt sometimes. But, we never . . . and, oh yes." He brightened for a moment. "There was Caroline, Ross Arnold's sister. Remember her?"

Alison nodded even though she didn't remember any Caroline, or any Ross Arnold for that matter.

"We went to the movies one night. But . . . I guess Ross was along that time. And besides, Caroline didn't like me. She was too young." He was looking more and more depressed.

"I used to watch Molly's grandma with you," Alison said, "when we'd all get together at school plays and stuff."

Oliver nodded.

"She'd stare at you sometimes with this kind of puppy-dog look in her eyes." She hoped she wasn't treating him like a child again. She didn't know quite what to say.

"Yes," he said, "I think I remember that too." He smiled then — a smile drained of regret. His eyes wandered back to the Theta Rae look-alike. "Let's go," he said to Alison. But not before giving the woman a wink.

Chapter 12

"WE'RE ALMOST THERE," Alison announced as they started looking for a good spot to camp out that night. They had exited from the thruway not long after crossing the Massachusetts border. A slim road formed a part in the lofty green mounds that the tourbook identified as the Berkshire Hills.

"Let's stop here for a minute." She pulled off the road and jumped out of the car to take in the view. Jogging up the road a bit, she felt more exhilarated than she had in days. "This is so . . . so absolutely gorgeous." She wanted desperately to share the scene with someone. A friend – Jordan, perhaps, or Molly. Someone to whom she could someday say "Remember those mountains called hills? Remember that feeling of being about five years old again and ready to take on anything or anybody?"

Oliver took his time walking to her side.

"Don't you feel great here? Take a deep breath. Think how far we've come?"

"Yes, it's nice," he answered. "But . . ."

"But what?"

"We've come far, yes, but we've got a ways to go."

"Oh, don't be such a fuddy-duddy." She took a long, deep breath as if to show him how it was done. The air smelled of moist soil and sun-baked leaves. Looking all around her, she felt a part of the green clan gathering formed by the tall, wildly irregular trees. She could have sworn they were whispering to her.

"Let's go, Chief," Oliver said.

When they returned to the car, she said, "Okay if you drive, so I can keep looking around?" She'd examined his face and posture; he seemed fit to drive.

"Not at all. This kind of driving I like. No line of cars a mile long to get in my way."

They drove in silence, Alison trying to look everywhere at once, desperate to slow down. But she left Oliver to drive as he wanted. His impatience was welcome after all his earlier weariness.

Sweeping around a wide bend in the road, they found themselves behind a flaking red pickup truck of uncertain make or year. Oliver grumbled and banged the heel of his right hand on the steering wheel. They had to slow down to thirty miles per hour, and there was no passing on such a curvy road.

Alison sighed with contentment. Molly would be the one, she thought, to share this with. She'd be eager to get out and tramp through the woods, moving fast and furious but always ready to stop and meticulously examine a wildflower, or to hold her breath when stumbling upon an animal. Alison felt badly about having suspected, even for a moment, Molly's motives in suggesting the trip to Rockport.

The red truck rocked and bounced ahead of them, a blond ponytailed head visible through the back window of the cab.

"She's having trouble handling that pile of junk," Oliver said. His hand hovered over the horn a few times, ready to blast the truck off the road if possible, but never quite going through with it.

"Don't follow her so close," Alison advised, but her real attention was elsewhere. "There are so many different kinds of trees all blended together here. Birch trees have to be my favorite, though. I mean, they're kind of scrawny, but the way the light plays around the white papery bark . . . I'm glad we're here in late afternoon; the light is perfect."

She unfastened her seat belt, pulled up on her knees, and bent over the seat to find her paper and pencils in the back seat. She wanted to have them ready next time they stopped.

Suddenly their car swerved sharply to the right, tires screeching. Oliver let out a yell, then sucked in his breath. She felt herself jerked toward him and then she grunted as the hard steering wheel pounded into one buttock.

As soon as they had stopped completely, a silence shoved its way into the car. Everything around them seemed to halt, to watch and listen. The birch trees huddled over Alison, their pale trunks soft as flesh. This isn't real, she thought. It's a picture, that's all. I've somehow crawled into a picture of an accident in the middle of the woods.

It was only after she stared at the red pickup truck in front of them, at an angle, that she realized that Oliver had simply stopped suddenly to avoid a collision. She pulled her leg free of his lap and turned to where he sat, his eyes open but dazed.

"ARE YOU ALL RIGHT?" The silence shattered. She hadn't meant to scream at Oliver but that was the way her words came out. "OLIVER — SAY SOMETHING." She turned his head so she could see the bump that was already beginning to grow ugly.

Sensing that there was someone in Oliver's half-opened window, she noticed out of the corner of her eye that it was a young man. He was saying something and she looked up to see that he had a blond ponytail hanging loosely to one side.

"Oliver, please," she begged. "Talk to me."

He took a few quick breaths and then wheezed. "Yeah . . . okay . . . stop leaning . . . it hurts."

"What hurts?" the young man asked. "God, I'm sorry. I was just trying to turn. I didn't realize you . . . what hurts?"

"My head," Oliver said, his breathing sounding more normal now. "Get the hell off me, Alison."

"He bumped his head," Alison added stupidly. "On the window."

Alison stared at the young man who'd been driving the truck as he examined Oliver's forehead. His hand suddenly extended toward her, brushing against her side, raising the tiny hairs all up and down her arms. But he was only freeing Oliver from the seat belt. "What about you?" he asked Alison.

She exhaled and tried to smile. "What about me?" Her voice was not her own, nor, it seemed, were her scattery thoughts.

"Are you hurt?"

"Oh, no. I hit my . . . I mean, I was turned the other way. I'm fine."

"Listen," he said as though speaking to a child, "that's my driveway I was turning into. Let me take you to my house. Laurie can look at him and decide if we should take him to the hospital. There isn't one for miles, you know. She can look . . . Laurie will know what to do."

The man helped Oliver to his truck and laid him gently

on top of some old quilts heaped in back. "Can you drive the car in?" he called over his shoulder to her.

She wanted to act helpless for some reason, but instead she settled in behind the wheel. Following the truck down the long dirt driveway to a crude cabin, she was grateful for the young man's decisiveness. A woman, presumably Laurie, emerged from the building. She was at least eight months pregnant.

"Chris, what is it? What's happened?" the woman called, running awkwardly to the truck. For several minutes they both hovered over Oliver, deft hands checking him here and there. Alison watched from the car, feeling achy, especially in her backside and legs, and very much alone.

I'll get out of the car, she thought. Then I'll know if I'm hurt. As she stood, she felt something like sand draining from inside her head. It filled up again and then drained again, repeatedly. Curling back into the car, she began to cry, for what particular reason she wasn't sure. Worry about Oliver, certainly. After all, they were almost there, almost to Rockport. What if . . .

The man's face returned to her window, still anxious but easing into an appealingly shy smile now. She tried to smile back, but knew hers was a teary, sloppy one.

"Want some help?"

She nodded.

His grip on her arms left tingly spots. Trying to clear her head, she focused on his hands. They were square and calloused, flecked with blond hairs and small pink scars. Hands that worked hard. Probably built the cabin himself. For her — that Laurie person, her belly straining against her flimsy peasant blouse.

"This young lady here's a little upset, I think," he said. "We better get them both in to lie down."

The woman nodded, holding a wet cloth to Oliver's head and stroking his shoulder tenderly. His eyelids looked blue and quivery.

Alison broke free of the man's grasp, cupped her hand across her mouth, and just barely made it behind a tree to vomit.

Alison woke up from her nap and tried to roll over before she remembered what had happened. At first she was sure she could scarcely move at all, but then she discovered that moving actually relieved much of the stiffness in her muscles.

She was in a small bedroom, on a hard bed that smelled of mildew. Otherwise the smells were soothing — freshly aired blankets, pine paneling, and melted candles.

Voices from the next room drifted in at about the same time as the rich smoky smell of pork frying. Her mouth tasted sour, but she doubted she'd ever been hungrier.

It was still not quite dark outside so she couldn't have been there very long. She heard their voices now, but not Oliver's. She had to find him, but the voices sounded so conspiratorial; they made her feel as if she should stay in the bedroom. Besides, she didn't want to be seen just then.

A small oval mirror hung on one wall and she took a tentative look at herself. Worse than she'd expected — skin the pale bluish color of skim milk, hair too awful to touch.

She sank back onto the bed just as the door inched open. "Hello," she said meekly. "I'm awake."

"Good." It was Laurie peering in at her. "Feeling better?"

"Yes . . . I guess . . . where's my grandfather?"

"Aha! I won the bet. I said he was your grandfather. Chris said great-grandfather."

"He looks older when he's not feeling well." Alison was annoyed at the idea of such betting. What else had they discussed about their two guests? Had they checked for identification? Wait a minute, Alison reminded herself, these are nice people. I should be grateful instead of getting suspicious again.

"Want something to eat? Your grandfather seems to be waking up too."

"Yes, thank you." Alison stood up and swiped at her hair with one hand. "Could I get cleaned up first?"

The light in the hall was dimmer, and then sunlight sprang into her blinking eyes when they entered the kitchen. Through a huge picture window Alison could admire the sunset and she gazed into its orange opacity for comfort. She didn't allow herself to look around, as if by not seeing the ponytailed man, she would be hidden from his view as well.

They had a surprisingly modern bathroom. She'd half expected to be sent to an outhouse since the cabin was so rustic and so obviously built by people unattached to luxury.

After washing up, she attacked her hair with a comb she found on a shelf among razors, shampoos, soaps, and insect repellents. Her dark limp hairs mixed with the long blond ones already in the comb. She slipped them all off and, unable to find a wastebasket, stuffed them in her pocket.

Laurie was at Alison's side as soon as she emerged from the bathroom. Cool fingers curled around Alison's upper arm. "I guess you've already met Chris. I'm Laurie," she said. "And your name is – ?"

Still suspicious in spite of herself, Alison did not supply her name immediately. But Laurie's brown eyes were encouraging, curious in a friendly way.

"Alison O'Brien. I'm awfully sorry about all this. My grandfather was driving too fast and following the truck too closely. He gets impatient sometimes." The effort of all those words uttered so quickly made her lightheaded. She felt a chair behind her urging her to sit, and she knew it must be him, Chris, who was holding it for her. Probably staring at her stringy hair. She said thank you without looking at him.

"You look beat, Alison," Laurie said. "And hungry. I'll go see about your grandpa."

"Please, don't . . . I mean, let me go. He's probably worried about me."

"Of course. Chris, show her where our room is. I'll put the food on in a few minutes." She turned back to Alison. "Okay?"

Alison nodded. "I'm so sorry," she said again, following the plaid-shirted back into the hallway. Chris was very narrow except for his shoulders.

"That's okay," he said. "We're glad to have you."

Oliver opened his eyes as soon as she entered the room. He gave her a quick, crooked grin and lifted one hand. She took it between hers and pressed it to her cheek.

"How're you doing, Chief?" he asked.

"Fine. How about you?"

"Headache. Otherwise fine. These folks have been taking good care of me."

Alison turned around, but Chris had left them alone.

"This beats camping out tonight," he said, "or another motel."

She sat up straighter, lifting her chin and lowering his hand. "We can't stay here, Oliver. What are you talking about?"

"Why not? I don't think I'll be up to much till tomorrow."

"They don't have the room here."

"They said they usually sleep in sleeping bags, outside or in the living room anyway, so that leaves us with two beds."

"They're just saying that to be nice."

"Laurie swore to it. Said sleeping on the floor is more comfortable for her, gives her back support."

"It's true." Laurie's voice startled Alison. "Come on now, supper's on. Can you make it to the table, Mr. O'Brien, or shall I bring you a tray?"

"No trays for me, little mother," he said, getting boldly to his feet and swaying only slightly.

Alison gripped his arm, a bit stung by his having a pet name for Laurie already.

Waiting for them at the table was Chris, who grinned and offered a chair to Oliver. Chris began to talk about his truck, trying to take the blame for the near-accident. As he spoke, Alison stared at him. Pitchblende eyes. Dark skin against hair and eyebrows the color of winter grass. His was, she decided, the most beautiful face she'd ever encountered. It filled her with longing and also with fear. She didn't know which feeling to trust, or whether she could really trust anything anymore.

Chapter 13

THE PORK CHOPS, steamed vegetables, and homemade bread arranged before them looked thoughtfully prepared, a meal for company, not for sudden intruders. But each forkful in Alison's mouth was off-tasting. She was sure it was only her nerves. Her stomach lurched up once when she gulped down half a glass of milk.

There were three faces eating near her, for the most part silently. Oliver looked pale but shoveled food in as though racing a timer. Laurie paused several times in between bites to touch, with one forefinger, her protruding stomach. Her long black hair parted in the center to triangulate her face. The tips of her cheekbones and an oval around her mouth were windburned, but otherwise her skin was a little too white. Alison realized that it was her broad, horsy smile that made it impossible to dislike her.

"Where're you two from? Somewhere in Minnesota?" Chris asked after pushing back from the table. "I noticed the plates on your car."

Alison nodded. "Alexandria," she lied, and Oliver's fork paused, but only for a moment. She waited for the next question, the one she'd been expecting.

"And where're you headed?" Chris seemed merely curious, not probing. His boyish smile — small even teeth, a laughline cluster above each high cheekbone — reminded her of one of the old pictures she had of her father. Or, she wondered, was that pure fantasy. Fantasies could be dangerous.

"Cape Cod," Alison answered politely. But she felt the cough that her voice was trying to smooth over, to conceal. She always felt like coughing when she lied — a dead giveaway. Oliver coughed for her, and she felt her throat open and warm to the task of continued lying. "My parents are vacationing there. I mean, we all are, but my parents flew out to be by themselves for several days before . . ." Her voice dwindled and she tried to stoke it up with more food.

Oliver sat, finished with his meal, waiting with the others.

"How nice," Laurie said to no one in particular, shifting a bit in her chair. "Romantic." She might have nudged Chris's leg with her foot because they gave each other secretive looks.

"Where are you meeting them?" Chris was beginning to sound more than curious.

"Cape Cod," she answered again, thrashing about in her imagination for some way to cut off his next question. Time. She needed time to think. And search the tourbooks.

"I know. But where in — "

"Hyannis," Oliver supplied. "At the Rainbow Motel, where they stayed on their honeymoon."

Alison almost cried with relief. Instead, from her chest rose a bubble that burst into a harsh choking cough, the one that had been hiding in her voice all along.

Laurie flew to her side and began pounding on her back all in one efficient motion. Nobody seemed to panic, but Alison felt the dinner spoiled. And it was her fault.

Eyes brimming and face hot, she finally stopped choking and excused herself.

The light knock on her door a few minutes later sent her into another search for details. Were they even on the right route to Cape Cod? Probably not. Sightseeing. That was it. They were going to Boston first. Museums and stuff.

But it was only Oliver. He looked weary; the purple lump on his forehead seemed to drag him into her room headfirst, arms and legs limply complying. "Ah, me." He shook his head and sat down next to her on the bed. "What am I going to do with you?"

"I had to lie, Oliver. They could call the police, or even Mom, if they wanted to. If they found out . . ."

"They don't care where we're from or where we're going. Not really. Just making conversation." He sat very still, looking around the room, which was partially darkened. The overhead fixture contained a naked bulb too weak to light a whole room.

"Are you feeling okay?" she asked automatically, but when he didn't answer she examined his face, trying to probe the wrinkles deepened by the improper light. He looked frail – and very old.

She pushed gently against his shoulders so he would lie back on the bed. His face could not seem to find a good, comforting streak of light, and she drew closer. "Go to sleep, Oliver." She stroked his forehead. "I'll take care of you."

He sighed and settled down into the quilt as she rose to her feet. Wishing she could hide in the room forever, she thought about drawing; but even that felt unnatural in this cabin where they didn't belong. They should leave. But Oliver had to rest. Another day or so according to Laurie, who seemed to know everything.

Alison opened the door slowly, soundlessly turning the knob. The hallway was dark and cooler than her room. A tunnel coolness. Again she wanted to hide, but she cleared her throat and ventured into the light. Laurie was still in her kitchen, seeming as much a part of it as her bulging belly was a part of her. She had pulled her hair back into a haphazard knot to do the dishes. She was clearly older than Chris. Alison figured her to be about her mother's age, only more naturally worn, more open about age than her mother.

Chris sat sprawled under the only lamp in the living room, apparently engrossed in a book. She could not make out the title.

Alison chose the kitchen. "Oliver's fallen asleep in my . . . in the room I was in. If it's okay, I'll just sleep in my sleeping bag. In the same room. I don't want to put you out."

"Fine," Laurie said with her smile at its broadest, practically straining her lips. "If it will make you feel better, but I wish you'd stop thinking of yourselves as in our way. We haven't had company for so long and I, for one, love it."

Alison nodded, picking up a rag to wipe an already clean counter.

"Tomorrow, if you're both up to it, we can talk and show you around this wonderful woods of ours. We own it, you know. Our own little hunk of woods. Chris used to work for this construction company not far . . ."

Alison stopped paying attention as Laurie rambled on. Was it her imagination or was Chris watching her? He hadn't turned a single page of his book since she'd emerged from her room.

A low, hollow moan sounded so suddenly that it took them all a moment to react. It could have been from outside, or even from another world. Laurie was the first to rush to the room where Oliver had been sleeping.

By the time Alison got there, Laurie was already mothering Oliver, wiping sweat from his face with a dishrag. Chris followed closely behind Alison.

"He gets these nightmares sometimes." Alison hurriedly tried to explain away the terror in his face and in his clawed outstretched hands. She wanted to push Laurie aside. Leave us alone, can't you? she would have shouted, but she could hear Chris breathing over her left shoulder. Calm. I need to be calm. As if this whole thing is nothing. "He was in the war, you know," she continued with a grave smile.

"I'm all right," Oliver mumbled, pushing off everyone with trembly fingers. "Please. I'm . . . leave me be."

Laurie herded them all out, lifting her towel as if to snap it at them if they disobeyed.

"Oliver?" Alison gazed at him over her shoulder, but he did not call her back to his side. Was it his head injury? Or, more likely, the little people again? Laurie and Chris must not find out about the little people. They'd think he was crazy for sure.

Laurie left the light on in Oliver's room. Alison did not bother to explain to her that light and dark had nothing to do with it. Moving in the same efficient, unchallengeable way she'd seen Laurie move, she went out to the car where she'd figured they had left her sleeping bag. She must try to stop explaining things in ways that might prompt more questions. Nightmares about war? Oliver had never fought in any war to her knowledge. Why not? It had never occurred to her to ask him.

As she extracted her sleeping bag and pushed the trunk door down hard against the cushion of air inside, she trembled. Then she knew why. A shadow floated closer to her.

"Can I help you with that?" Chris asked. When he stood by her, she realized he had to be at least half a foot taller than she was. In her entire grade at school there were only a few boys who were that tall, and they were mostly basketball players who slouched too much.

"You going to be a senior next year?" he asked as if having read her mind about school.

"Uh . . . yes. That's right." Let's see, that would make me sixteen or seventeen, wouldn't it? I'd have my license then. Clutching her sleeping bag between them, she wanted to get past him and into the cabin. As nice as he was, he made her strangely uneasy, though she figured it was just his looks, and his casualness. She, meanwhile, had broken out into an embarrassing sweat, which she was sure he could detect.

"Anything else you want to bring in? How about this art stuff? Yours?"

"Yes. But no. I mean, no thanks. This is all I need." What's the matter with me? she wondered. Why is it so unbearable to be alone with him like this, in the dark? Briefly she thought of Jordan and how safe he made her feel when they were alone together. But then it occurred to her that the comparison was ridiculous.

"Well," he said, turning to climb the wooden steps, "you probably better get to bed then. You've had quite a day."

Inside, Alison said good night, politely, to both Chris and Laurie. She sounded to herself like a child saying nightie-night. Now I lay me down to sleep . . .

Oliver was wide-awake when she entered the room, obviously waiting for her.

"Were they here tonight?" she asked, dropping her sleeping bag. "The little people?"

He nodded.

"We'd better go then, first thing in the morning."

Oliver did not respond.

"Don't you think?"

"I think," he said, "we have to stay. They want . . ."

Alison remembered what Mira had said about trying to talk him out of his fantasy, but she couldn't think how to do that without raising her voice. She longed to be alone with him again, and on their way. "Oliver, we will stay only long enough for you to rest up. Plan on starting out tomorrow, late morning, okay?"

She found Laurie's rag and put it back on his forehead, then sat down by him. "Tell *them* that, if you have to. Be firm and strong with them." She paused. "Like you used to be with me when I was a nasty little kid. Remember?" She poked his shoulder with her fist. "Remember the time I decided to starch the laundry so I could make clothes-sculptures?"

He grinned and moved to his side, cuddling the pillow. The rag slid off his head.

"You were so mad I thought you were going to starch *me*."

"My longjohns never recovered," he said with only a hint of the old anger.

"They were my best work, Oliver. What a great sculpture that was. The plaster I added was the secret. And the flesh-colored paint."

"You wrecked my best longjohns." He closed his eyes and his eyelids flickered. "The ones I used to go hunting in with old . . . Arnie . . . Johnson."

She sat by him until she was sure he was sound asleep.

Chapter 14

*W*HEN SHE AWOKE the next morning, she thought she was in her own bed at home, then in a motel room. But moving her limbs slowly, she felt the hardness of the floor beneath her and smelled the pine paneling of the cabin again.

Keeping her eyes closed, she wished she *were* back in her room. She had dreamed of a tall blond man with a ponytail, who had started dating her mother and then, characteristically, had been told to shove off. Brokenhearted, he'd turned to Alison for comfort and they'd ended up kissing, right in the middle of her mother's clean yellow kitchen.

Oliver groaned and sneezed somewhere above her. She opened her eyes to dust balls skittering across the floor under his bed. He was thrashing around as he often did when trying to wake up.

She sat up tentatively, trying out her back, and realized that she had actually slept quite comfortably. More so, she suspected, than Oliver had. Slipping on her clothes, she made a dash for the bathroom, positive she was the first one awake. She winced at the noises she made in there; the cabin seemed to be constructed of cardboard for all the privacy it afforded. Mumbling and giggling sounds reached her from Laurie and Chris's room, along with the harsh clear sounds of drawers being shut. Oliver groaned again.

By the time she had showered, borrowing whatever she needed rather than going back for her suitcase, Laurie had nearly finished making breakfast.

"You look fresh this morning," Laurie said with a grin.

"I'm feeling much better, thank you," Alison admitted. "And I think Oliver is, too."

"I hope so. He didn't sound that great during the night. I was reading something about nightmares recently . . ." She paused, a spatula in midair, waiting for the recollection before returning to her pancakes. "Well." She smiled. "I guess it was about children's nightmares."

"He's certainly no child," Alison said, trying for the tone of a joke but sounding instead rather snotty.

"No, I guess not." Laurie flipped the pancakes with the same ease most people achieve turning the pages of a book.

"And he hates being mothered," Alison continued.

Laurie just gave her a strange look.

Alison was reminded of her mother. "I really couldn't eat a thing," she said.

"Nonsense." Laurie's hair, which was styled differently somehow, was filtering sunlight in distinct layers. The top wayward hairs stuck out as yellow filaments, while the next layer drew only a few brownish-red flecks from the sun, and the bottom thick layer remained impenetrably black.

Alison looked around her. "I'm sorry about hogging the bathroom. I wasn't thinking, I guess."

"There's always outside," Chris said, entering the kitchen

from the porch, scratching his bare chest. He wore only cutoff jeans and Alison shivered. Her eyes wandered up from his chest to his hair. It hung long and fluffy in tiny sharp waves, the kind that can only be achieved by braiding. All night in braids. She realized then that Laurie's hair was similarly kinked and puffy. Alison pictured them last night, braiding each other's hair before going to bed. Long fingers separating and caressing each soft strand, that tickled their palms. She felt herself blush.

"You're embarrassing Alison," Laurie scolded her husband.

He moved close to Laurie's back and reached around to touch the tight package of belly that was his baby. Then his hand slipped back and lower to rest on her hip. Their bodies fit like two bowls nesting together.

Alison swallowed. Is this what it felt like to watch your own mother and father loving each other?

Laurie made an exaggerated move to stack the pancakes, releasing Chris's grip on her. "Alison here says she's not hungry. See what you can do to change her mind, honey."

Chris looked at Alison for the first time that morning and a liquidy feeling spread inside her chest.

"Well," she said to distract herself from his dark, inquisitive eyes, from the teasing mouth, "I suppose I could eat one pancake."

"Is your grandpa awake?" he asked, passing by her and lifting a single finger to flick at her dripping wet hair. He smelled of perfumed handcream.

"No. Yes. I don't know." Alison rushed back to the room where Oliver was nearly finished getting dressed. Her heart pounded and she was afraid he could hear it.

"Morning," he said, looking about as gloomy as she'd ever seen him. "Suppose you want me to get ready to go."

"Well, I don't know." Alison didn't want to leave just yet; the scent from Chris's hand clung to her hair.

During breakfast, Alison kept glancing at Oliver, then at Chris, and back again. Why didn't somebody tell her what was happening and what she should do? She was tired of being in charge of the trip and longed to be taken care of for a while. Maybe just for one day.

Alison tried to help with the dishes but Laurie shooed her out of the kitchen. Oliver sat in an old wooden rocker, which began to creak rhythmically. He stared straight ahead, out the window into still leaves.

"It's such a beautiful morning," Laurie practically chirped, "why don't you go outside, have a look around, Alison? Chris will give you the grand tour."

"No, that's —"

"Sure, let's go," Chris said, gently squeezing her wrist between his thumb and forefinger. "Come on. There's lots for a young artist like yourself to absorb. Maybe you'll sketch the place for us."

"How'd you know I'm an artist?" she asked as he coaxed her through the door and down the steps.

"I saw the stuff in your back seat. Remember?" He glanced at her and added, "I wasn't snooping, honest."

She blushed.

"Would you, then? Sketch our house? It would mean a lot to Laurie. And me."

"Sure." She looked around. "I'll wait till later, though. The light will be better. More even."

"Fine." He showed her his carpentry shop. His rockers and bookshelves looked fine and sturdy to her, but Chris scoffed at them. "Tourists love handmade things from New England. I give them what they want — junk boxes mostly." He held up two small wooden boxes, scarcely large enough to hold anything but buttons.

"What would you rather be doing?"

He looked at her with a frown pleating his perfect tanned forehead. His long hair parted in the middle to form the kind of double arch she used to use to depict birds flying in the distance. "I'm not sure. That's the truth. And with the baby coming and all, I seem to be getting less sure all the time." He shrugged and left the shop without her. She spotted a tiny wooden box with a carved leaf design surrounding a curlicued letter *A*. She tucked it inside her moist palms and followed him back toward the cabin.

"I'll trade you," she called after him. "This box for my sketch. If—" she caught up to him and blushed "—you like the sketch, of course."

He did not seem pleased about her finding the box. "Junk," he snorted.

She smiled up at him. "It's almost as if it was made for me. I love it."

He looked amused and irritated at the same time. "Well, then, it's yours."

She followed him back into the cabin and found Laurie and Oliver exactly as she'd left them.

"That was quick," Laurie said, drying her hands. "Didn't you make it down to the gazebo?"

"Not yet," Chris said, and closed himself into their bedroom.

"Moody," Laurie said. "But then I'm sure you understand. You artists are all pretty moody, aren't you?"

Alison outlined the *A* on her box with her forefinger. She thought about showing it to Oliver, but he was still rocking and still glowering. So she put it away with her things.

Laurie was making bread and she clearly wanted to chat. She couldn't seem to stop, filling the cabin with an aggravating kind of buzz that began to give Alison a headache. Alison didn't, quite frankly, care what they decided to name the baby, nor whether the kid would be taught at home or risk the corruption of public schooling. Alison wondered if Laurie had any friends or anyone besides Chris to talk with.

During a pause, Alison jumped in. "I'd like to walk around the cabin now, I think. Before I start sketching it." She glanced at Oliver, but he had no apparent reaction.

"Fine," Laurie said. "Do you need my help? No, I suppose not. I'll leave you alone." She turned back to the glob of sticky dough her hands had disappeared into and began to hum a tune.

Alison crouched down to Oliver. "You going to be all right?"

He nodded and looked straight at her, but said nothing.

She hesitated for a moment, then escaped the sounds and smells of the cabin as she walked into the warm summer moisture outside. Gnats hung around her head in a loose net, and the more she batted at them with her hand the more dense the net's weave became.

Circling the cabin proved to be more difficult than it had looked because of tangled underbrush and leftover piles of partially sawed lumber. The cut wood had been soaked through by rain and had taken on a delicate layer of moss; it was already beginning to merge once again with the woods. Contenting herself with only one time around, she pulled her sketchpad and pastels from the car and settled down about seventy-five feet from the cabin along the driveway. What she wanted to sketch was Chris's face, but she resisted and began with the frame of pine trees around the cabin.

When the sketch was nearly finished, she heard something behind her and jumped to her feet. It was Chris. She hadn't even noticed him leave the cabin, she'd been so absorbed in her drawing. She guessed she loved the cabin nearly as much as he did, now that she'd found the slope of its lines, poked into all its careful angles.

"That's really fantastic," he said, peering over her shoulder. "I had a feeling you were talented."

"It's not quite finished."

"Maybe not, but you've captured it. You really have."

She tried not to tremble as he watched her apply the last few touches, removing the sketch from the pad and handing it to him.

"I really thank you."

On an impulse, she asked him to sit still for a few minutes and she sketched his portrait. She did this less to impress him than to ease the dull ache she'd been feeling, the need to try to put his face on paper. When it was finished, she was embarrassed; it was not an objective portrait at all. She saw immediately that it showed all his perfections and none of his flaws. She had observed the way his nose humped, not quite in the middle, but she had not put that in her picture.

He looked at it a long time, without comment, and then rolled the two sketches up and touched her elbow. "For this you deserve the rest of the tour." He led her down a path that ran perpendicular to the driveway and away from the cabin.

The gazebo appeared suddenly like a surprise about a hundred yards down the path. It made Alison think of merry-go-rounds, in this case a small wooden one. There were no horses or music, but she was as enchanted with it as any child about to pick out the best horse on which to ride.

"It's nice, isn't it?" Chris said. "I built this last year, the one thing I've been proud of since the cabin." He led her to an elaborately carved bench, just big enough for two thin people, and he sat down. After a moment's hesitation, she joined him, on his left.

Across a shallow valley, she could see a picture-postcard view of the Berkshires — hundreds of green cotton-candy trees, all different shades. Their foliage was so thick that Alison could almost feel the shadowy chill from the underside.

She felt his arm next to her on one side and the arm of the bench on her other side. It was a cozy but strange feeling that made her sigh, and then shiver unexpectedly.

"Cold?" he asked. He was still holding her rolled-up sketches with his right hand. Occasionally he bounced the roll on his knee.

"No. Just . . ." She examined the width of the bench. "Does Laurie even fit in this now?"

"Only by herself." He unwedged his arm from between them and rested it in back of her.

He has put his arm around me, Alison thought. Or has he? Her skin prickled with the feeling that he was about to touch her in some grown-up way, or maybe even bend his head forward to kiss her.

She listened to his breathing next to her and then cautiously glanced at his face. But she might as well have been ten feet away from him; he was smiling dreamily, still surveying the view, still sharing the beauty of it with a "fellow artist." That was, she realized, all he meant to do.

With a hot rush of embarrassment, she stood up and

moved away from him, away from his breathing and from his hands. She'd made a fool of herself; she'd misjudged someone again.

"Had enough?" He was looking at her with curiosity and perhaps with amusement. She wasn't quite sure. What did his look mean? What did *any* look mean, she wondered. All she knew for sure was that she'd been flirting with him, practically since she'd met him. My gosh, she thought, he's almost old enough to be my father. There it was again — that dreadful emptiness where a father should have been.

"What's wrong, Alison?" Chris seemed genuinely concerned, maybe even a little frightened. He drew his left hand into his lap and glanced at it. With his other hand he squeezed the sketches.

Alison realized he must have been wondering if he'd done something to offend her. "Nothing." She shook her head. "Nothing's wrong, really." How could she begin to explain to him her confusion about men, especially about fathers?

"I don't know what's the matter with me," she added quietly. When she saw his puzzled expression, she turned and began to run back to the cabin. The gnats found her again; one flew into her open mouth and another one got caught in her right eye. She blinked and she wanted to cry. But she couldn't give in to that now. It was time to leave.

Alison saw Laurie standing on the porch, arms folded and supported by her belly. She was rubbing one upper arm and waiting, unsmiling. "Where's Chris?"

"Is there something wrong?" Alison asked guiltily.

Laurie looked beyond Alison, into the trees. "I'm not sure. Maybe I'd better go find Chris, though."

Alison felt alarm rising up, yeasty and unrelenting as

Laurie's bread dough sitting on the windowsill. She watched Laurie thread her way through the woods.

"Oliver," she called even before entering the cabin. The living room was empty. "What happened in here? Oliver?" She tried the door to the bedroom where they'd slept. It was locked, or barricaded, she couldn't tell for sure.

"Oliver, it's me. Open the door. Please. I'm here now. I won't leave you again. Just open the door."

"I didn't mean to grab her. She was in danger." His voice came from the other side of the door. She could almost feel his breath on her face. "I *thought* she was in danger."

"Oliver, open the door."

"She got so scared of me. I tried to explain it wasn't me but *them* she should be afraid of."

Alison heard Chris and Laurie's voices outside. She thought they'd said something about calling authorities.

"Oliver." She tried to be calm, in charge. "We have to go now. Let me in so I can get our things out to the car."

After a scratching sound around the doorknob, Oliver's face appeared in the opening crack of the door. It was the same face she'd grown up with, practically the first face that meant anything to her. It had hovered over her crib right from the beginning, even more than her mother's. It had often showed her if she should be smiling or frowning about what was going on around her. She smiled now, and that apparently comforted Oliver enough to open the door all the way.

She wrapped her unsteady arms around his neck but only for a moment; she knew how he felt about hugging. Her tears had forced their way out and her smile felt pasted on.

"We've overstayed our welcome," she said.

"So it would appear."

Chris stood inside the front door with Laurie behind him. "I think we'd better get someone here," he said. "To help you, Mr. O'Brien."

Laurie moved to her husband's side then, looking a little sheepish for trying to hide.

"No," Alison said quickly. "We've been enough trouble for you already. We just need to be on our way again. Oliver . . . he's fine. I'll take care of him. I always . . ." She left them to gather her and Oliver's belongings, pausing only long enough to examine the initialed "junk" box and then shove it into her purse.

Their baggage was bulky, especially with her hastily rolled-up sleeping bag, and she decided to make two trips to the car. Oliver followed her out on the first trip, and climbed slowly and a bit unsteadily into the front seat of the car.

"Are you okay?" she whispered through his half-open window, but he didn't seem to hear her. "Oliver?"

"I'm just so . . . embarrassed. Please, let's go."

She patted his shoulder and returned to the cabin for the last suitcase.

"Wait now." Chris stared out at Oliver and rolled the sketches in his hands tighter and tighter. "Laurie," he said, "he grabbed your arm, didn't he? And shoved some furniture around?" After a meaningful look from from Laurie, Chris lowered his voice and turned to Alison. "That doesn't seem quite normal, does it? Somebody should be notified."

Laurie sat down with a grunt. "Oh, let's not overreact. They'll be joining her folks soon. Right?" she asked Alison.

Alison nodded uncertainly, only vaguely remembering the lie she'd told.

"It's not really our business," Laurie continued, "what they do. He was probably just having another nightmare.

He could have been asleep in that chair. I don't know." She sighed and added, "I'm so darn tired all of a sudden."

Chris stood by his wife, gently caressing her shoulder while he thought things over. This gesture made Alison's stomach tighten, and she knew she was blushing again. She wondered how she could even have thought Chris was attracted to anybody but his wife in "that way." They were husband and wife, adults, and she was still only making believe. She realized with tremendous relief that he'd probably been totally unaware of what was on her, Alison's mind.

"Here," Chris was saying to Laurie. "Put your feet up. Get some rest."

Alison finished loading the car and then awkwardly approached Chris. "Thanks a lot for your hospitality. I'd like to pay you . . ." She unfolded a twenty-dollar bill that had been in her pocket, but Chris waved it away and pointed to the sketches as payment enough.

"Have a safe rest of your trip," Laurie said with a weary smile.

Alison glanced at Oliver sitting in the car, perfectly still and staring straight ahead. She thought he should say good-bye and thanks, but she decided not to press her luck. He was, after all, right where she wanted him — in the car and ready to go. So, after a quick good-bye for them both, she joined her grandfather, and they were off once again.

Chapter 15

"YOU'RE MAD AT ME," Oliver mumbled. "Don't deny it, you are mad."

Alison had not denied anything, but now she felt obliged to do just that. "No, Oliver. It wasn't your fault. Come on, perk up. We're out of there now." When he didn't respond, she wondered if he had been talking to the little people, not her.

He was looking bleaker by the minute. His skin matched his hair, which blended into the pale sky. With his eyes averted, there was no color at all to his face. Out of the corners of her eyes, she sensed his slow fading. A bright plaid shirt held up by air.

The scenery of western Massachusetts breezed by her now, mostly unnoticed. The vast wooded hills, previously so seductive and beautiful, now seemed to secrete wooden cabins and pursuing "authorities." She'd left the turnpike and had found an alternate, more northern route. It was a smooth, winding two-lane road.

The whole scene in the gazebo skimmed by her, along with the blurring trees. Had she simply been in love with

Chris's physical beauty, she wondered? Like romances she'd had in the past with works of art? Or was there more to it than that?

Alison forced her thoughts away from Chris, and back to safety. She and Oliver were headed for Rockport now. That goal had seemed to slip to one side for a while, as if the town itself had slid into the ocean. Her father waving and smiling, smiling and waving as he got smaller and smaller. And then swallowed by watery distance. She knew the feeling well. It was, in comparison to what had happened that morning, something she could handle.

She knew now that her expectations had loosened to accommodate whatever her father said and did. She would accept whatever he gave her because that was all he could give. If he asked her to stay with him, great; if not, that was okay too. They could talk a lot, learn each other's faces, hug. No, he probably wouldn't be any more of a hugger than Oliver, but that was understandable, forgivable. Maybe she could simply concentrate on his talent. Their shared talent. That might be enough. If they could only work together . . .

A gas station and café appeared conveniently at noon and Alison pulled into it a little reluctantly. She'd wanted to be closer to the coast before stopping, but she and the car both had urgent needs. The gas tank got filled first and then she bought some take-out food. Oliver left the car only long enough to go to the bathroom. He said he wasn't hungry but he ate a sandwich anyway, nibbling tentatively into the middle of it and leaving a crumbly smile of crust.

The sun was high and hot now, and Alison longed to lie down in it for a while, draw some color from it. But another glance at Oliver tugged her back on course.

No unnecessary delays. She could get a tan by the ocean, couldn't she? Go sightseeing later?

"Hang in there, Oliver. I just saw another sign for Boston. We're not far now."

"Boston? I thought we were going to your dad . . . to Rockfish . . . Rockport." The confusion in his eyes frightened her enough to pass two cars of sightseers. In one sat a young couple, the wife's left arm draped over her driver-husband and her right one gesturing with a crumpled map.

The other car's back seat contained two small children, their heads bouncing in and out of view rhythmically. Alison imagined them whining "Are we almost there, Mommy?" and "Where's the ocean, Daddy?"

The father, she noticed in her rearview mirror, spoke around a cigarette clenched in his teeth, gangster-style. He'd be uttering "Sit still," and "Shut up," and other such endearments. Or maybe — she smiled at the thought — cigarette or no cigarette, he might be telling them all about the ocean they were approaching. The way the waves collapse your knees and knock you over. The way the saltwater stays on your tongue, and bakes into a film on your shoulders.

Who had told her these things? She narrowed her eyes and bit her lip. Molly's father? Oliver? Her mother? Maybe she'd only read about the ocean. But she decided that the father with the cigarette was filling in, for his children, the blank spots left by books. Maybe a confrontation with a baby shark, harmless and pettable. All animals were cute as babies, weren't they? Even sharks.

Oliver snored and then sneezed explosively. He did not wake up to wipe his upper lip.

She had loved this old man more than anyone, except her mother, for years. But now he slumped in a heap at her side, runny-nosed, sick, and terrified, holding her back. She wanted to hug him and comfort him, while at the same time, she wanted to deposit him in the nearest hospital and be on her way, lighter by a ton.

Such awful thoughts creep in when you're driving, she told herself. Occasionally she had even wondered if her arms, on their own, might now jerk the wheel to the left, right into an oncoming car. Could arms do that without specific instructions from the brain?

"Boston sixty-eight miles," she said out loud to clear her head. "Boston cream pie, Boston baked beans, Boston . . . White Sox — no, Red Sox — Boston Massacre, Boston Strangler — ugh! Boston Bridge, no, that's Brooklyn Bridge." She laughed loud enough to wake up Oliver if he'd wanted to wake up.

She glared at him. He would have been able to provide dozens of Boston phrases. If only he would talk to her now — smile a little, joke, tease her. She knew she was being unfair and unsympathetic. But nobody, at the moment, was being particularly fair or sympathetic to her either. Her arms might jerk the steering wheel at any time. Then they'd have to call her mother: "There's been an accident, Mrs. O'Brien . . ." "Oh God, no. Not . . . oh, my baby. Oh, Alison, what have I done?"

At the funeral, their caskets would be side by side, clunky handles nearly touching. An old man and a young girl. She watched the funeral service — a detached observer, a journalist at a tragic event. The picture began to jiggle, a television fadeout. Then there was just the road ahead. A sign. Boston sixty miles.

"Boston Tea Party," she said triumphantly. "Of course." This time Oliver's eyelids flickered, and he readjusted his skinny shoulders and his mouth in a way that looked more like himself. He seemed about to clear his throat, open his eyes, reach across the seat and comfort her. It was so possible that she felt it happen, even though he went back to sleep. He had helped, just enough. And she would help him, of course. It was not really in her to do otherwise.

"I love you, Oliver," she whispered so she wouldn't disturb his sleep.

Mother, mother. Darling daughter. Don't go near the water? What, she wondered, was that from? She must have been wondering out loud because Oliver supplied her with the answer.

"Mother, may I go out to swim? Yes, my darling daughter. Hang your clothes on a hickory limb and don't go near the water."

"What a strange nursery rhyme that is," Alison said. "I never thought about it much before, even though it was one of Mom's favorites, wasn't it?"

"I think so. It seems to me to make perfect sense, though. Coming from a mother."

Alison thought about that until a road sign snapped in and out of view. "Oliver, check that map again. Isn't it around Lexington we're supposed to get off two and get onto one twenty-eight going north, away from Boston and toward Gloucester?"

He looked. "Are we on two or two-A?"

"I don't know for sure, but that sign back there said something about Concord and two-A. I'm turning around."

"We should be on two-A, I think."

They took the turnoff to Concord and it was clear from the start that this would just bring them to the center of town. But Alison stretched the mistake out a bit. "Look, Oliver — that sign says this is the way to the house Louisa

May Alcott lived in, and look at that house over there. What does that sign say? My gosh, Oliver. The history in this town. Look how worn the sidewalks and steps are. Imagine all the important feet — "

"Turn around up there now, Alison. We've got to get back to two, the few miles more to Lexington."

"Couldn't we stop just for a minute?"

He grunted. "Within an hour or two of Rockport and you're suddenly interested in Louisa May Alcott and Nathaniel Hawthorne — "

"I've always been — "

" — Revolutionary War battles, and worn sidewalks." He sorted and swallowed his pills, right on schedule, she noticed. And he was trying to sit up straighter, to keep his chin higher. He was rehearsing, she realized. He did not want to be sick in Rockport.

Alison sighed and turned around, away from Concord, and toward the correct route.

Oliver nodded approvingly. He hadn't mentioned the little people since leaving the cabin, and she hadn't asked. Whatever had happened back there with Laurie would be locked away as safely as her disturbing encounter with Chris. No sense bringing up bad times when they'd left them behind simply by climbing into the car and zooming off. Route 128 turned out to be a multilane highway, They'd make great time now to the ocean. "But don't go near the water." Alison smiled to herself.

It was after about twenty minutes on 128 that she saw the police car. The siren was not sounding, nor were the lights flashing, but it was behind them, sticking pretty close. Careful to stay exactly at fifty-five, she changed lanes a few times. Sometimes the policeman changed lanes also, sometimes he didn't. But he was always in her rearview mirror somewhere. Could be coincidence, she thought. But when a turnoff presented itself, she decided to test the patrol car. Sure enough, it turned also, but still there was no other apparent interest in Alison's car.

"We stopping?" Oliver asked.

"I have to find a john." She decided not to mention the police car to him. Maybe he wouldn't notice. Or maybe she was just being paranoid again.

"I guess I could use some food, come to think of it," Oliver said, trying to stretch kinks out of his legs. "Maybe ice cream?"

"There must be an ice cream parlor in a town this size." When they found a Friendly's, she parked the car across from it on the street, reluctant to let the cop know where they were going. She almost cried with relief when the police car drove slowly on.

Inside, they were surrounded by women and children of all descriptions. A child of five was running and trying to slide on the floor even though it was carpeted. None of the women seemed to claim him enough to bother with reprimands. An elderly woman watched the child suspiciously and mumbled to herself. Her skin looked as fragile as rice paper, but her ink-colored eyes had the open vitality of a child's. Alison would have liked to hear what she was saying, but didn't want to intrude. The running child began a new game, arms spread, chocolatey mouth buzzing like a World War II–movie airplane.

Oliver reacted to the children much the same as he had at the oasis a few days earlier — with wary distance. It was strange because he'd always loved little kids before. Alison left him for the bathroom, feeling confused but still relieved about escaping the cops . . . until a few minutes later, when she made the connection between children and little people.

Hurrying back to Oliver, she realized she was already too late. She heard him before she could see him, crouching in a corner booth, under the table except for his head and arms. "Alison. Alison!" He was calling her name in a high, pathetic voice.

"Oh, no. No, no, no." Her heart felt as though it might pound right through her chest; the sound of it, and Oliver's cries, were all she could hear.

An arm from somewhere tried to keep her from the booth, but she shrugged it away. Four other arms were beginning to touch her grandfather, causing him to crouch lower, cry louder. Still she could not hear other voices, but she sensed their interference, along with that of the determined, intrusive arms, pulling her, pulling and poking at Oliver.

Somehow she reached him at last, and she freed him from the arms and from the booth. His muscles were rigid, his body stiffly resisting, and she couldn't seem to keep a good grip on him except in his armpits, which were damp and hot. The feel and smell of him brought her other senses back to her.

"We're just trying to help, miss," an attractive woman in jeans was saying.

"Did you call that ambulance?" another, more distant voice said.

She started to sweat, too, but was determined not to cry or in any way let the people think she needed their help. She focused on getting Oliver out of there, back to the car, back to safety with her.

"We're halfway to the door now, Oliver. Hang on. I'll get you there. One step, two steps, that's right."

They made it out the door, leaving a whispery crowd behind. "There's the car, across this road here. See it? Let's hurry."

But there, in the middle of the road, Oliver stopped. He was planted as rigid and solid as a statue. Cars slowed and honked, veering around them at the last minute. She felt the rush of air pass them and smelled the exhaust. She couldn't seem to breathe properly. "Oliver, come on. PLEASE. Move. We can't stop here. MOVE." She tugged on his arm, pushed, pulled. Everything she did seemed to make him worse. He was petrifying in that spot. In the middle of a road.

One of the cars did not try to go around them. It stopped and a middle-aged man in a business suit ran to them. "Here, miss. Let me . . ." The man, with a concerned smile, loosened Alison's grip on Oliver. "He on some kind of medication?"

She shook her head and then nodded vigorously. Was this man a doctor? He started counting to Oliver, slowly. How did he know Oliver was taking medication? Was he talking about drugs? Her grandfather wasn't some kind of junkie. He was a respectable elderly man. She grabbed his arm again and the man, still counting and comforting Oliver, once again pulled her hand loose.

She could not hold back the tears any longer. She wiped at her face, trying to think what she was supposed to do.

More counting from the man, and this time it worked. Oliver was across the street in the next few seconds.

"I'll get him to the hospital," the man said.

Someone else said something she couldn't understand. Everything seemed to be softening – even the pavement beneath her feet. Softening and blurring. She followed Oliver into a car. Whose car is this? she wondered, and then curled up in the back seat, letting them do whatever had to be done, just so Oliver would be all right again.

Chapter 16

WHENEVER ALISON had been in hospitals before, she'd thought they smelled of smuggled-in *dirtangerms* — a word she'd coined as a child. It reminded her of when she used to crawl into a bed of crisp linen after she'd played outside all day and forgotten to take a bath. "Dirtangerms, dirtangerms," she'd sung to herself until the bed felt less forbidding. Now she closed her eyes and held tight to that child in her head, the one that had nothing to do all summer but play as hard and as long as she could.

"Miss."

She opened her eyes and blinked into the fluorescent light above the waiting room.

"You can see your grandfather now." It was a nurse speaking.

Alison followed the slim white back to an examining room. Oliver was sitting up on a table, but when he saw her, he jumped off and bowed.

"Oliver, what on earth are you doing?"

"I'm fit as a fiddle."

"Come on. Sit down. Nurse — help me get him to sit down, won't you?"

"I'm telling you, Chief, I'm fine." But he did sit down.

"What did the doctor say?"

"He'll be back in a minute," Oliver said. "He's ordering up some more tests, which I'm going to refuse, however."

The nurse shook her head and left them. Did her expression spell out "crackpot," Alison wondered. Or was it more a look of admiration?

The doctor entered then. He was a small, jovial man with a gray crewcut and pink cheeks. "Hello," he said and extended his hand to her.

She nodded as she shook his small, warm hand. Finally, she blurted out, "What's wrong with him?"

"Well . . ." He and Oliver exchanged looks and she could have screamed with impatience.

"It was my sneeze pills, Chief."

"What?"

The doctor went on to explain the hallucinatory effect of combining anti-Parkinson's medication with antihistamine. "Not uncommon. We see drug-induced hallucinations so often they're easy to spot. Your grandfather has responded extremely well to our efforts to treat the imbalance. But — " He seemed to force himself to turn somber as if he had just been nudged with a cautious reminder. " — we want to make sure that's all that's going on."

"Of course it is," Oliver said. "I'm fine now, and I know what to do differently. So we're going, Doc."

"Listen to me." The doctor was having trouble restraining his smile. "I've conferred with your physician in Minneapolis, and she agrees that these tests should be run. Maybe you should even stay the night, just to be — "

"Hell, no. My son is waiting for us. And besides, I don't care what that doctor says. She was just trying to cover her tracks because she never thought to ask me right out about my sneeze pills."

He turned to Alison. "It never occurred to me to mention my allergies to her because it was fall at the time, and I've been taking those things so many years, I've stopped thinking of them as medicine."

Alison nodded, still confused. A few hours earlier, it had appeared that Oliver was crazy. That she'd lose him. At least for a while. Oliver's doctor in Minneapolis must have called Alison's mother by now. I should probably call Mom too, she thought. But that would have to wait. She stared at the doctor, trying to make sure she wasn't misinterpreting anything. "You mean, he'll be fine as long as he stops taking the pills."

"No, no. He has to keep taking the anti-Parkinson's pills. Absolutely. But we've got things readjusted, chemically speaking. And, yes, of course, no more . . . sneeze pills." He and Oliver shared the joke enthusiastically.

She wanted to laugh along, but she felt so stupid. It had been such a simple mistake. But it had nearly cost them so much.

Returning to her chair in the waiting room, after they'd forced Oliver to have those tests after all, she repeated the last words he'd said to her: "We'll be out of here momentarily. Wait for me."

"Miss." The same nurse was at her side again. "Give me your car keys. Mr. Atkins is seeing to it your car gets here safely. It'll be in the back parking lot."

"Oh. Here? Our car? Thank you." She handed over the keys. "Thank him. Thank . . ." She felt suddenly bathed with relief. There are such nice people in the world, she thought. She wanted desperately to stand up, find the man and thank him herself. Had she even been civil to him before, in the car? But her legs wouldn't move.

Sitting back in the chair, she drifted into a dreamy nap. She was about seven years old. The most important thing just then was finding a caterpillar. Just the right caterpillar. She was going to keep it and watch it spin its cocoon. Even if it took weeks of watching. Her mother was trying to explain to her why it wouldn't work, how she was sick to death of hearing about it, and would Alison please stop crying and grow up, once and for all.

"There it is."

"I see it. My gosh, how could I miss it?"

They'd turned a corner, faced a sudden, grand expanse of ocean, and Oliver had stopped the car. In the distance, dozens of sailboats, like white moths, flitted across the gray water.

"Thank you, God." she whispered, her eyes filling with tears. "And thanks to you too, Oliver, for letting me talk you into taking this route. The slow route. So I could see . . . this."

They had left the hospital in similarly good spirits and found Route 127, the coastal route out of town, headed toward Gloucester and Rockport. Oliver insisted on driving, even though it made her jumpier at first. She kept searching his eyes, dissecting his sentences, for signs of something. What? More weird people, maybe giants this time?

Alison, faced with the ocean at last, was afraid to blink for fear it would vanish. But when her eyes blinked on their own, nothing changed. She and Oliver were there, both of them, at the edge of the land. And the people around them, on the sidewalks and streets, acted as though it was nothing — just a body of water. So what if it dwarfed

144

people to the size of microorganisms, and its depth paralleled the height of the grandest mountains?

Oceans mean beaches — that's what the people around her seemed to concern themselves with, nothing more. A mother grasping hold of a toddler's hand and tons of beach paraphernalia crossed the street in front of them. The little girl cried when the hot pavement stung her bare feet. The mother's arm circled the little waist, hoisted her up and added the child to her burden like an extra blanket. At the corner sat a teenager with a cardboard box labeled "FREE KITTENS. Black and White." The little girl screamed to be released when she saw inside the box, but the mother trudged on toward the beach.

Oliver started the car again. "There's only a few miles between Gloucester and Rockport," he said. "And that sign said eleven miles to Gloucester."

Alison gave him a disappointed frown. "Couldn't I just stick one foot into the water? One finger?"

"Later. Eleven miles on this little, slow-poke road will take forever as it is. Don't make me stop just so your finger can have a dip. Patience, Chief."

She oohed and ahhed at this quaint little church with the picturesque steeple and that ancient, palatial home. And always noted each glimpse of sea.

"Guess you'll be filling your sketchbook tonight," Oliver said.

She nodded, but then wondered. Tonight still seemed a continent away. Anything could happen yet. "You know, I think if I'd talked to Mira more, about your pills I mean, she'd have figured out what the trouble was. She seemed very suspicious of those pills, now that I think about it." Why wasn't I? she wanted to add. Suddenly she laughed.

"What's so funny?"

"I was just thinking about how Mira would laugh at our stupidity right now if given half a chance."

Oliver laughed too.

"Let's go find her in New York," she said, feeling suddenly so free and unencumbered she could even find a tiny speck of a person in that immense city. As easily as the gull she was watching could find what it wanted in the ocean.

"Alison."

"I know. I know."

He shook his head. "I don't understand you sometimes."

She glanced at him. "Do you feel kind of grimy? Like we've been traveling across the desert or something? I sure wish we could get cleaned up before we see Dad." She reluctantly turned her gaze away from the soaring gull. "Hi, Dad," she practiced aloud. "You don't know me, but I'm your little girl."

"You worry too much," Oliver said. "Always have."

She sighed and pulled from her tote bag a crumpled piece of paper and stared at it as if it revealed the future. "Dad's address. I think it's a boarding house. He mentioned a Mrs. Stanisch a couple times, said she owns the place."

"We're all set then," Oliver said. "When we get there, we'll ask directions from someone."

"All set," she said and swallowed.

Oliver was able to drive straight through Gloucester only after promising Alison they'd come back later to explore, and perhaps to paint. To her, the town appeared to have been pulled right out of a book about the sea. Even paintings she'd seen of fishing villages hadn't prepared her because they could only hint at the sounds and smells. She never would have thought such a strong fish smell could be so enticing. She'd never known that the ocean, with all those people crowded on its edge to force their living out of it, could have such a strong voice of its own – not just gulls, waves and wind, but a true gusty voice.

They drove on, their eyes continually darting to the right, toward the sea. Oliver drove very slowly; he seemed excited in a festive, can't-wait way that made Alison feel lonely. She wanted to feel excited too, but she couldn't quite shake the feeling of unreality. If she were to get excited, she felt, she might end up making a fool of herself.

When they entered Rockport and the traffic became heavier and the air more congested, Alison asked Oliver to pull over and stop. He complied and they sat together in the hush of expectation, scarcely breathing.

"Alison," he began, "do you remember that time you unplugged the clock to stop time?"

"Sure I do. I was about five or six, wasn't I?"

"You stopped the clock at four thirty-six so your mother would not be able to come home to start dinner and find what you'd done in her oven."

"That's what I thought would happen, sure. In my feeble little mind. But of course she came home anyway and saw all the Tupperware melted into green and white goo, stuck to her oven racks."

"A fearful sight indeed," Oliver added, chuckling.

"I just wanted a pet so badly and she always said no. So I thought if only I could try to hatch all the eggs from the refrigerator, warm them up, surely one of them might make it. Why I picked Tupperware to put them in, I'll never know." She looked down at her hands, which curled limply in her lap.

"Stopping time didn't work then and it won't work now," he said. "Being almost there has felt so good, so full of possibilities. Better, perhaps, than . . ."

"Than what we'll find when we get there?"

He nodded.

She turned her face up to his. "All of a sudden I'm so afraid." She saw that he felt the same way.

He nodded again and switched on the ignition. "We're here now. Let's go see what we came all this way for. Okay, Chief?"

She sat up straighter, combed her hair, even dabbed on a bit of powder, mascara, and lipstick. She forced her hands not to shake; the lipstick must look as though she wore it all the time. Her face, in the rearview mirror, appeared older, wiser. "Okay," she said.

Chapter 17

ALL THE TRAFFIC was headed for the same area of town, near the wharf, where shop after shop and gallery after gallery awaited them. The one thing that they couldn't see was a parking place. The road wound back after a while, away from the wharf. And there was still no place to park. All the buildings seemed to be leaning forward, toward the water, pinching off sidewalk and street space; and yet people spilled all over the area, walking in front of the cars, distractedly eyeing the next shop down the line from them.

"Have you spotted his street yet? It's not really such a big town." Oliver was poised over the steering wheel nervously.

"No. What we need to do is park and then ask directions and see about walking there. You up to that? You look tired. In fact, you don't look so hot, to tell you the truth."

"That's just what I needed to hear, especially from the vision of loveliness sitting at my side. Maybe I should put some lipstick on."

"Oh, that's a great idea." Alison giggled. "Gosh, this isn't anything like I pictured a New England town to be. It's pretty enough, but it's so . . . ."

"Touristy. It looks like *it* paints on false faces too."

"Will you be quiet about the makeup already. Oh, look! That car is just pulling out. Grab that parking spot."

It felt so good to get out and walk, Alison didn't care how far it would be. It was a hot sunny day but cooled somewhat by the ocean breeze. The gulls were crying off in the distance; it sounded to her as if they were calling for help.

They headed back for the wharf because that's where all the people were. Many of them wore rubber flip-flops and carried folded lawn chairs like handbags. The vast beach area was colorfully spotted with people, few of them venturing into the water. "It's icy—want to stick that foot in now and see?" Oliver asked, testing her, she thought.

"Later."

They asked a proprietor in the first gallery they came to, and he gave them the simple directions. It wasn't far.

"Is it one of these gallery-type places?" Alison asked.

"No, I doubt it," the man said. "Not on that street."

"We're looking for Gerard O'Brien," Oliver said. "Maybe you know him."

The man shook his head but then appeared to think it over, just for the sake of politeness. "No, can't say that I do. I'm lousy at names, though. Faces, now, that's my thing." He swung his bare, deeply tanned arm around, indicating his gallery full of portraits.

"Thank you kindly," Oliver said, and they turned away.

Alison realized that she'd liked the proprietor immediately. It felt good to be less suspicious, less ready for conflict with someone when it wasn't necessary.

The building was old and windworn. Alison's heart was pounding and she had to keep wiping her palms on her jeans. Would they shake hands or what? she wondered.

150

The woman who opened the door was not smiling. She was tall and angular as a scaffold. "Well, well, well. It's the old man and the little girl."

"You weren't expecting us?" Alison felt her legs begin to buckle. She straightened them, moistened her lips, and cleared her throat. "Were you?"

"Oh my, yes. I'm Mrs. Stanisch. Gerry told me all about you after he got the call. Well, I'd overheard it anyway. That was, let's see, two nights ago."

Alison's heart stopped pounding; in fact it seemed to stop altogether.

"The call?" Oliver asked. His voice sounded cold, distant.

"Yes, from his wife. Ex-wife, I mean."

Alison looked at Oliver, who said, "Is he home now, then? Can we see him?"

"No, he's not here."

"Working somewhere — ?"

"He's split." At this the woman chuckled and finally opened the door for them. "Come in. His stuff's still here, of course."

Alison walked in on numb legs, block feet. A thick, musty, fishy smell hung from the ceiling like a curtain. She wanted to find the bathroom.

"Here," Mrs. Stanisch said, placing an envelope in Oliver's hand. "For you. And this one's for you," she said to Alison, clearly enjoying herself now. "I feel just like one of those M.C.'s on a game show." Her teeth, when she laughed, looked seashell brittle. "His room's number three upstairs, next to the bathroom. Prime spot, he has. Here's the key, if you want to have a look-see."

"Is he coming back?" Oliver asked. The corners of his mouth were twitching.

"Oh, sure. Sooner or later. He'll have to get his stuff,

won't he? And besides, this is the closest thing he'll ever have to a home."

"But," Oliver continued, his voice somehow steady, "he'll wait until we're gone?"

Mrs. Stanisch opened the palms of her hands upward as if to free the answer to that question from them.

Oliver nodded and, envelope in hand, headed for number three upstairs. Alison followed. She wished she could grab onto his hand. She blinked several times and then kept her eyes closed, pausing on a step. Oliver grabbed her hand then and pulled her along.

Gerard's room was tidy, partly because he'd obviously been packing and partly because there wasn't much to pack: a stack of canvases leaning against the wall; an ancient easel; an open suitcase piled with blue workshirts and ragged jeans; two cardboard boxes, one small and one large. The small box was filled with stubs of charcoal and pastels, balding paint brushes, stained rags, paint tubes squeezed nearly dry, a cheap child's watercolor set.

Alison heard Oliver ripping open his envelope. She held hers in her hand. It was marked, simply, "Alison." Oliver's note must have been brief because he quickly wadded it up and sank onto the bed.

"What does it say?" Alison asked. She was not crying, she noticed proudly. But she could barely feel the paper between her fingers. It felt about a quarter of an inch removed from the surface of her skin.

Oliver did not answer. He just sat squeezing the wad of paper tighter and tighter.

Alison decided to read hers. She knew that she would keep it for a long time, so she opened and unfolded it carefully. Regardless of what it might say, she could not destroy it the way Oliver had destroyed his.

Dear Alison.

Well, this is where I've been staying for the last couple years. That much of what I told you was true. Otherwise, it was all lies. My paintings haven't been selling, I haven't been teaching kids to draw, I don't even have the kind of friends I told you I did. This is it, kid. Nothing much to share with you, except what's in the big box, which I'm sure you'll recognize. If you can ever forgive me for leaving you again, then leave me the box. I'd like to be able to keep it forever. Maybe even add to it, if you're willing to send more. But if you must take it back home with you, I'll understand. It doesn't really belong to me anyway.

Love.

He didn't sign it. She figured he didn't know how to sign it. His other letters had been signed "Dad" but this letter, of course, was different.

Refolding the letter and stuffing it back inside its envelope seemed to take an hour. Her fingers trembled, her eyes focused and unfocused to some erratic rhythm, maybe her own pulse. Dropping the envelope near where Oliver sat, she dug her fingers into her eyesockets and then rubbed away a stickiness from around her mouth. Boxes. Where were those boxes? What big box did he mean?

She found it and discovered a puffy stack of paper inside, on top of which was a watercolor painting of Lake of the Isles. The sky was wildly multicolored and her signature, the one she used to practice tirelessly (simply "A. O'Brien"), ran up the bottom-right-hand corner.

Beneath that picture was one she'd recently done of her bedroom window, just the window, curtainless and slightly smudged. But inside the careful, detailed window frame were briskly sketched hints of the view outside – the delicate splayed needles of the white pine, a nest of grackles, the drab roof of the garage, a corner of the yellow daffodil bed, and just a few slivers of sky filling in spaces.

Her eyes filled with tears because it was then that the only visible painting in her father's stack registered clearly. It leaned against the others, shielding them from view. It was a painting of a window and the view beyond, borrowing everything from her painting except . . . except what? She couldn't put her finger on it, but there was something missing in his painting. Something approached and then backed away from.

She stared at this painting for a long time before returning to her own pictures in the box. Below her first two she found a backward progression of dozens of others, dated only by her ability. After the first several pictures she'd gone beyond those which she herself had sent him. One after the other she pulled them up, holding them against her stomach to see the next one down.

When she'd reached the bottom quickly, she realized with great surprise that her mother had been sending pictures since Alison was scarcely old enough to hold a crayon. She started through them again, this time from the earliest ones, which were simply geometric shapes with eyes, arms, and legs. The drawings progressed quickly into her tree stage – not the green balloons atop stiff brown columns, like those of her friends at the time. Her trees had sprawling, leafy arms stretched out from trunks that seemed to be racing on root-toes to grow bigger and get somewhere. Then the birds began. First they populated the trees, then they left the trees behind to perch on nearly everything Alison learned to draw. The birds grew more and more lifelike with time until their legs looked delicate enough to snap and their liquidy eyes seemed to wink.

Alison left her box to examine the rest of her father's paintings. She felt like a sightseer in her own life. In her father's life. Behind the window picture were several of a long red building on a dock, which was labeled Motif #1 and which she recognized because it was the one landmark in Rockport she was aware of—one of the most frequently painted subjects in the world.

Her father's paintings were good, but unremarkable. He'd also painted a few portraits. One, marked "Self-Portrait, 1974," showed a young man's face only; he had hair curling over his prominent ears, a serious mouth and frightened eyes. She was touched by the self-portrait, especially when she recognized the nose and jaw line as belonging to Oliver. She searched the expression for something of her own face and failed. She'd never noticed it much before, but she resembled her mother after all.

Her mother. Mrs. Stanisch had said she'd called. "I can't believe she did this to us," Alison said at last, leaning the canvases back against the wall.

"She?" Oliver still sat on the bed, and still held his crumpled ball of a letter.

"I can't believe she called him. She warned him. What a—" Alison left the room and found a pay phone down the hall.

She reached her mother at work, insisting it was an emergency. "Mom? This is me."

"ALISON. Thank God you're all right! I've been worried sick. Where are you?"

"Don't you know?"

"What's the matter? What did he say to you?"

"Who—the phantom father? You knew he'd split. You called him to warn him that we were coming."

"I . . . I . . . he's gone?" Her mother's voice became more muffled and Alison could picture the way she always stuck her forefinger across the length of her lower lip when she was upset. "Honey, I . . . honestly thought he'd be there. I only called so he wouldn't embarrass you both. With some friend, or something. And so he could clean up and look nice."

"How long have you known he was here?"

"Honey, I always know where your father is. We talk on the phone every now and then. Did you imagine that he could father my child and then vanish completely from my . . . from our lives?"

"I don't know what I imagined." Alison felt anger sifting out through the tiny holes in her certainty about the way things were. Her mother had only wanted to help? To make sure he was presentable? What kind of person was this man?

"Mom, he left all his things here because . . . well, I'm not exactly sure why, but he has a box of my stuff. All the pictures you've been sending him and I didn't even know it. I just . . ."

"Alison, can't you come home now? Please? Leave him be for now. You belong here with me."

"And Oliver?"

"Yes, of course Oliver. How is he? My God, I just got the call an hour ago from his doctor. She said you two were at some hospital. Is he okay?"

"Yes, he's great. He had to get his medication adjusted is all. It's a long story."

"You're coming home, then, as soon as possible? I miss you so much, honey." Her mother was crying and it gave

Alison an ache in the middle of her chest. "You know," her mother laughed hoarsely, "this may be a stupid thing to say to a runaway child, but I'm rather proud of what you've done — gotten all the way there on your own. And took care of your grandpa too."

"We took care of each other, Mom. And — " she paused to find the exact words she wanted, " — and other people helped too. More than you might expect."

"Well, anyway, I don't think I could've done what you did," her mother said. "That doesn't mean I'm not angry as well, though. Angry as hell."

"I know, Mom. I'm sorry."

"Honey, listen. Just jot down my charge card number, and, uh, call the . . . Boston airport and make reservations. No, wait, I'll do all that. You just drive there and fly home. Right now, you hear?"

"I can't leave the car, Mom."

"Why not? Who cares about the car? I want you two home and it will take forever for you to drive all this way again."

"Mom, stop crying, and be reasonable. I'm not about to leave our car here. I mean, there'd be shipping costs and everything. We'll drive home."

There was a pause while her mother cleared her throat. "I guess you're right. Oliver was always a reasonably good driver, and I suppose his license is still valid . . . let's see . . . it was three — no, four years ago that we had it renewed."

Alison gave a sigh of relief. So Oliver had had a license all along.

"But," her mother continued, "there's so much I want to say to you and I don't know if it'll keep."

"It will. I've got a lot to say to you too. Mainly, I guess, that I'm sorry. For lots of things." Alison started winding the telephone cord around her finger. "I don't know what got into me, but I wanted Dad so much, I couldn't think straight. And then, when it looked like Oliver was going away too, I . . . I panicked."

"I know, Alison. I should have known all that. I should have helped you understand about your father. And I don't know how I could have . . . started to slap you like that. Forgive me?"

"I do, Mom." Alison stared at the tip of her finger, which was turning purple from the tightly wound cord. "Well, I guess you better get back to work, huh?"

"Jordan's been calling."

"He has?"

"He's hurt that you didn't confide in him."

"I couldn't. You two have gotten so chummy, I was afraid — "

"We're *not* chummy, Alison. For heaven's sake, why do you insist on seeing it that way?"

Alison could tell her mother was trying very hard to keep her anger in check.

"He likes you so much and you hardly even notice."

"Oh, I noticed," Alison said. "I was afraid, though." She could hear Mrs. Stanisch's distinctive voice greeting someone downstairs. For an instant she wondered if it could be her father.

"You were afraid of Jordan?" her mother asked.

"Of getting involved with a boy. He was, oh, I don't know, starting to get to me. You know what I mean? I was starting to feel things for him. Maybe that's one of the things I wanted to talk to Dad about. I wanted to hear his side of things. Especially about boys."

"You should've said something to me. I might've told you that to get anything, you have to take risks, or something like that. Something I keep forgetting myself. . . . Listen, honey, I've got to go. They're really giving me the evil eye here. I think they're already figuring out how much to deduct from my paycheck for this call."

Alison laughed. "I love you, Mom." She didn't want to forget this time.

"Love *you*, honey. See you soon."

Alison returned to her father's room. Pacing back and forth on the creaky wood floor, she felt a jumble of sadness and gratitude and anger. Mostly she felt let down. "I'd like to pound him," she said. "I'd like to just see him long enough to pound him."

She pulled out his self-portrait from the stack and leaned it in front, where she could see it from some distance. Her anger began to feel pure and solid, like the residue left at the bottom of a strainer. The direction of it was so clear, she was afraid she might end up kicking in the self-portrait, so she turned away from it. "You'd think he'd at least be curious about me. You'd think he — "

"Alison, shut up." Oliver had not moved in all that time.

She sat down by him. His words did not startle her as much as the expression on his face. That doctor, she thought, was wrong. He looks terrible. What do we do now? But then she noticed the wadded-up letter in his fist and pried it loose so she could read it. It wasn't a letter at all. It was a bill, for the rent that was due.

"That's all I get," Oliver said, his voice squeezed dry. "After all this time. Not even a quick 'Hi, Dad,' or — " he swallowed " — even a 'Hello, you old s.o.b., you lousy excuse for a father.' Not even that."

Alison realized that she might have lost her father again, but Oliver had also lost his son. She'd nearly forgotten. "Oliver. I'm so sorry." She noticed he was staring at her father's self-portrait. "He got your nose and your jaw line," she said. "That's about it."

They sat together for several minutes in silence, in the room that was empty of all but a few fragments of Gerard O'Brien.

Chapter 18

O LIVER PAID the rent, of course, and that entitled them
to spend the night in Gerard's room. "We better
sleep good tonight," Oliver said. "Tomorrow morning we
head back."

They ate a supper of potato chips and soda pop because
that was all they felt like eating. Neither of them spoke of
Gerard all evening, even though his belongings kept
reminding them of why they were there. Alison decided to
leave the box of her pictures for him to keep. But there
would be no more sent. Well, probably not. In exchange,
she decided to keep "Self-Portrait, 1974."

They went out to breakfast early the next morning,
choosing a place overlooking the ocean. The sun was so
bright on the water that Alison had trouble keeping her
eyes open. After breakfast they leaned against a worn white
fence beside the cove. It was peaceful that early – no tourists
struggling with unwieldy packages, no sunbathers out yet,
no children crying in the heat. Only the sun and a few boats
on the water and the blue-white gulls not far above it.

To their right was most of the town, crowded onto a

peninsula. Out of the middle of it stuck a huge green-domed church steeple with a gold clock, from which sounded metallic chimes — Alison counted eight. 8:00 A.M. At the top of the steeple stood a weathervane, much like those she'd seen on all the other old churches they'd passed. And yet each church seemed to proclaim its history in a unique way.

Oliver sneezed several times, but he didn't seem to mind that he couldn't stop the sneezes with pills. It served as a reminder that he was in pretty good shape otherwise. He hummed the Hallelujah Chorus, softly, so as not to break the sunlit peace of the moment.

"Why do we feel so good this morning, Oliver?"

"I think it has something to do with what always happens after hitting bottom," he said.

"I hope we can keep it up then, because it's a long way from this beach to Minneapolis."

"What did your Mom say last night, by the way?"

"Oh, that she was mad but relieved. And proud — she said I'd done something she couldn't have done."

"And how'd she feel about Gerard?"

Alison squinted at a pair of plump children who were staking their early, privileged claim on the beach. They were followed slowly by a man who did not seem to be joining in with their fun. He had a look of aloneness about him. She didn't know how her mother felt about that strange, hurtful man, her father. "Who knows?" she said at last.

"She's probably feeling guilty somehow," Oliver said. "Gerard's good at making people feel guilty over his own actions. Last night, all I could think about was what a lousy, rotten father I'd been to him. Never there when he needed me. Never showed him that I loved him, even. No wonder he turned out to be such a terrible father himself." Oliver sneezed again. "That's where the guilt came in. I blamed myself for his running out on you. But I'm all through with that. Enough's enough."

Alison noticed the two children now running toward the water and the man watching them, one hand on his hip, the other one shielding his eyes from the sun's glare.

"It's like you," Oliver was saying, "blaming yourself for crying too much at night when you were a baby. Ludicrous. He didn't leave because of you or me, he left because of who and what he is. He simply never grew up, that's all. And I'm tired of feeling guilty."

Alison listened to Oliver and nodded. It was so rare for him to speak so long and so earnestly about his own feelings that she did not want to halt his voice with her own. Besides, she couldn't stop watching that man out on the beach. There was something odd about him, and every now and then he seemed to glance at them. But maybe it was just her imagination.

Oliver followed her gaze to the man on the beach with his children and shook his head. "You're searching still," he said. "I was hoping . . ."

"Oliver—" She found her voice creaky as if from the punishing ocean air. "I've been wanting to ask you something."

"Shoot."

"You said Mom and Dad had to get married because she was pregnant. That was an accident, obviously."

"Obviously."

"Well, then that baby . . . never made it, but Mom got pregnant again with me, soon after that. You'd think they'd have . . . well, been more careful by that time."

"I wondered about that myself," he said. "Gerard, now, of course, blamed your mom for getting pregnant again.

As if he'd been out of the country the whole time."

Oliver gazed out to sea as he remembered. "They fought a lot while she was carrying you. But it was mostly the same old stuff. Just more intense because of losing the baby, having another one on the way, and all that. It was a terrible time for them. I'll never forget it. It's no wonder, when you think about it, that you were such an unhappy baby. Everything improved after he left. You stopped crying so much and Tess was practically her old self again."

Alison remembered the old Tess as they'd been talking about her earlier on the trip. Long parted hair, open pretty face. Her future had been breaking into pieces in front of her, but her face didn't show it, at least not in any of the pictures from that time. She looked, Alison thought, determined. Always determined.

"I asked her once," Oliver continued, "when you were about a year old, I think. Gerard was long gone by that time. I asked her if they'd been careless again, having you. And you know what she did?"

Alison shook her head.

"She laughed in my face. 'Are you kidding?' she said to me. 'I wanted this baby more than I've ever wanted anything in my life.' That's what she said. And then she told me, more than college, more than a home and a marriage and all those things, she wanted a baby. I think she'd known for a while that she and Gerard wouldn't make it. She knew she wouldn't have much time, so she got pregnant again as soon as she possibly could. Before her husband could leave her for good, all alone."

Alison's eyes stung with tears.

"It was you she wanted," Oliver said. "If she could've figured out a way to make you twins or triplets, she'd have done that, believe me."

164

"Then why," Alison whispered, short on breath and fighting the tears, "does she seem to need so much more lately? I don't make her happy most of the time. That's for sure."

"Because you're growing up. That's why. She's letting go, just as she should. Well, maybe not as gracefully as some, but she's had to do things the hard way. So now she's got some catching up to do. Don't make it harder than it is, Alison. We've both got to give her more freedom from now on."

Alison nodded but then gave him a quick, panicky look. "Does that mean you're leaving us after all?"

He shook his head but it did not seem to be in answer to her question. His look was distant; it matched the sounds of water and gulls.

"Oliver, you can't. You just can't."

He shook his head again.

She needed to tell him something, she knew, but she couldn't find the words until she recalled what he'd said earlier. "Oliver, you said you'd been a lousy father — "

"Lousy, *rotten* father," he corrected.

"When you said that, it didn't sink in right away, what it was I needed to say back to that. Oh God, this is coming out all messed up. What I mean to say is that you got a . . . a second chance and you did a terrific job."

He pulled his attention away from the gentle waves and the crying gulls.

"With me," she continued. "You were *my* father. I don't know why I was too dumb not to just leave it at that. But . . ." She wanted to hug him so bad her arms ached. Instead she wrapped a hand around one of his long forefingers. She knew what he'd say next.

"Such small hands," he said softly. "You always had the

smallest hands. The way they wrapped around one of my fingers, in the park, in a crowd . . . hanging on tight. Like we were plugged into each other." He rested his chin against his chest, his eyes closed. "Of course, I won't leave you."

"Good. That's settled."

"But *you* will be leaving before long, you know."

"I know, I know. But that's different. Maybe you can come with me. Maybe we can head back out here when I'm done with school. You can fish, I can paint."

"And —" He opened his eyes and looked at her, hard. "— we can find Gerard once and for all?"

"No, no. I don't know. . . . I suppose that would be nice, but it doesn't really matter much anymore." She squeezed his finger once more and then let go. "Come on," she said. "Mom's waiting for us."

They turned away from the beach and back to the car. Back to the same stretches of turnpike and highway, the same kinds of rooms and restaurants. But Alison began to see *this* journey like something she'd turned right side out. They wouldn't be saying "we're almost there" anymore; soon they'd be saying "we're almost home."